CALLING CARD . . .

Jeffrey Scott Duncann leaned back in his executive, leather desk chair and examined the chipped, blue-flint arrowhead that had just been delivered to him. The heavy-set man shook his head in confusion. What in the world was an Indian arrowhead doing on Westerly's desk? It didn't make sense. But the more he thought about it, the more he remembered an old newspaper story. It was about a do-gooder, part Indian, who had developed a career for himself charging around the country battling against all the bad guys he could find. Some strange name they had given him . . . yes, the Penetrator.

J.S. let his eyes go wide in surprise. Here? The Penetrator was interested in this little scam? Impossible. But Westerly had been as frightened as a man could be. He wasn't faking it. He must have met this Penetrator face to face. At least he lived to talk about it. Most people didn't.

This had to be kept quiet. J.S. did not want the press to pick up the story or it would be blown all out of proportion and GTA would suffer. Unfortunately, this Penetrator wasn't the kind of man you could call up and bribe, or even reason with. In fact, nobody knew who he was or where he lived. He just turned up where the trouble was. So how did he happen to land in Hollywood? That Rolls Royce over the cliff? The newspaper reporter spread all over the freeway? Violence had drawn the Penetrator to Hollywood the way blood in the ocean pulls in sharks from miles around. The same genuine killer instinct. . . .

THE PENETRATOR SERIES:

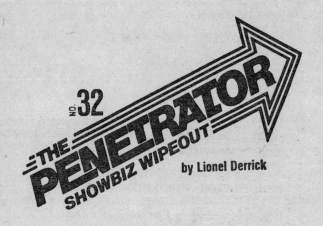

THE PENETRATOR

NO. 32

SHOWBIZ WIPEOUT

by Lionel Derrick

PINNACLE BOOKS   LOS ANGELES

PENETRATOR #32: SHOWBIZ WIPEOUT

Copyright © 1979 by Pinnacle Books, Inc.

An original Pinnacle Books edition, published for the first time anywhere.

Special acknowledgment to Chet Cunningham

First printing, July 1979

ISBN: 0-523-40514-6

Cover illustration by George Wilson

Printed in the United States of America

PINNACLE BOOKS, INC.
2029 Century Park East
Los Angeles, California 90067

TABLE OF CONTENTS

SHOWBIZ WIPEOUT

PROLOGUE

Howard Goodman sat at his desk in one of the FBI offices in Washington, D.C., and stared down the row of small cubicles with their seven-foot-high glass and metal partitions. He felt like an animal trapped in some pristine zoo. Howard let a burp of pure stomach gas course up his throat. He scowled. He felt as if an acid convention were holding a rock session in his gut.

Goodman looked down at the notes on his desk and swore silently.

The Penetrator. The damn Penetrator was at it again, and just today the Bureau had pulled him off his special assignment. Before he'd had carte blanche to go hunt down this Penetrator terrorist and nail his hide to the courthouse wall. Now the special duty was over. He was grounded. The director had given Howard a year to capture and charge the Penetrator. Instead Howard had produced nothing but wisps of gray smoke, testimonials, and a few near misses. The man even had been on the FBI's most wanted list for a month.

Hell, the damn Penetrator was a menace. He was a goddamned killing machine. Goodman had traced forty-seven outstanding murder complaints against the

Penetrator. Besides, there were thousands of minor charges, plus over a hundred felony complaints against him, involving illegal weapons, kidnapping, and assault and battery, leaving the scene of a crime, and unlawful flight to avoid prosecution. Goodman had a big file case almost filled with complaints, cases, and reports on the man who they still knew only as "The Penetrator."

He was the egotistical son of a bitch who went around leaving blue-chipped flint arrowheads on his victims. He was a blatant show-off, a publicity hound.

In his search Goodman established that the Penetrator began five or six years ago in Los Angeles. There he wiped out half of an important Mafia family. Goodman wasn't worried about saving organized crime members, but it was still illegal to kill even them unless you wore a badge and had just cause.

From that first hit, Goodman traced the Penetrator's journey through Las Vegas, New York, Chicago, Tokyo, Canada, Florida, the Bahamas, Denver, Seattle, Mexico, and dozens of other places. Thirty-one times the Penetrator had struck, leaving death and bombed buildings behind him.

Always it was the same. The man swept into town, attacked or killed someone, violated someone's civil rights, wound up killing up to three dozen persons, who were usually described as local criminal elements, and then—after the situation was resolved—the Penetrator left town before the local authorities or the FBI could get on the scene and make the Penetrator accountable for his actions in a court of law.

Goodman grimaced as his stomach produced another jolt of acid. What hurt Goodman as much as anything was that this Penetrator had never taken his lumps. He never had to come up on charges for excessive force or the use of a firearm in a dangerous situation. Never had the Penetrator stood up to a Bureau or Department shooting inquiry. All normal law enforcement agency men had to stand for a shooting inquiry. It simply wasn't fair, goddammit!

Goodman was five-nine and about one-hundred-sixty-five pounds. He had blond hair, blue eyes, and fair skin. Howard was thirty-four now, and his total goal in life was to nail the Penetrator and make him stand charges. This guy operated outside the law and got away with it, and the blatant unfairness of that infuriated Goodman almost beyond endurance.

Now the Director personally had stripped Goodman of his special assignment to catch the Penetrator. Goodman went back into the national pool of specialized agents in Washington to be assigned to any field job that fits his talents.

But the damn Penetrator was running around loose with nobody even on his case!

It wasn't right, and there was no way Goodman was going to sit on his tail and let it happen. He'd go see his section chief and work right up the ladder to the Director himself. Howard stood quickly and walked down the aisle between the rows of offices toward his supervisor. But as he went, he walked more and more slowly until he at last veered off at the drinking fountain, took a long pull of the cold water, and stalked dejectedly back to his desk.

Goodman stared at the sheaf of data he had collected on the Penetrator. He didn't even have a reliable name on the man. The Penetrator seemed to use a different alias on each mission, and usually Howard found different fingerprints as well. That was impossible. To top that, the fragment prints they found never matched up with any known prints on file. It was amazing. After considering the fingerprint problem for almost a year,

Howard at last decided that the Penetrator must be wearing some kind of skintight plastic gloves with partial prints somehow built into the gloves in an infinite variety. Nothing else made sense.

After more than a year on the case, the data file was embarrassingly thin. Howard had no name or prints, not even a good physical description. Tentative ones listed the man as from six-feet even to six-three, with dark hair, dark eyes, a brownish or tan complexion with perhaps part-Mexican or part-Indian blood. He had just about tied down the Penetrator's home base. Howard guessed it had to be on the West Coast and probably in Southern California because of the man's constant tan. But if the Penetrator were part Indian or part Mexican, the "tan" would be meaningless, region-wise.

Howard threw his pencil down on the desk and scowled. What he hated most was when the newspapers called the Penetrator a modern-day Robin Hood. A man who helped the poor and downtrodden, who fought against crime.

Hell, the Bureau had been battling crime for fifty years, more or less, and they never got any good press notices like that. It was a mockery of the whole justice system.

Goodman stared at the stack of file folders on his desk. He had a few cases already, and now the deluge would never stop. He'd be working fifty or sixty cases soon and be so swamped he'd never see the site of another Penetrator strike again.

Howard spent another hour thinking about the chances he once had to catch the Penetrator and at least to work out his operating methods. But no more. The damn do-gooder had a reprieve.

"Do-gooder, ha!" Goodman mumbled. The man was

a threat to society, a cold-blooded killer. Howard knew the Penetrator had army training because of the service weapons he used professionally. The Penetrator even used military tactics and strategy.

Goodman had often described the Penetrator as a "goddamn gun for hire." Right now the maniac was taking his licks against the criminals, but what happened when somebody offered this Penetrator more money to change sides? Then this same bastard would be gunning down civic leaders, captains of industry, taking pot shots at Congress, maybe even going for the President himself!

Goodman slumped at his desk and stared at the file folder in front of him, but he wasn't reading a word. He had only one purpose in life now, and that was to bring this fanatic called the Penetrator to justice, to tree him, and put him in front of a judge and jury. Only then would Howard Goodman be able to sleep nights.

Chapter 1

NO, NO, NEVER!—YES

Melissa Martindale wished Susie were there, or Helen, or the maid. Someone. She didn't like to be alone in her big Topanga Canyon house, even for a few hours. Today it had just seemed to happen that way. Susie, her cook and housekeeper, phoned early to say her car had not one but two flat tires, and it would take her all morning to get tires changed and repaired. It was the maid's day off, and Helen had to go into Universal for a nine o'clock appointment with that new producer. No one ever had a better agent and personal manager than Helen.

Now Melissa bit her lip, wondering. She had just pushed the buzzer opening the big gate for a TV repairman. He said someone called for service this morning. A momentary memory of the Sharon Tate murder flashed through her mind, but she pushed it aside quickly. One couldn't be frightened all of one's life and keep tucked away, hidden from the public. Melissa's million-dollar smile faded to a frown. On the other hand nobody had told her any of the TV sets needed fixing. Oh, well, it would be all right.

Melissa Martindale was a true Hollywood star. At age thirty-two she was on the top, a fragile, classic

6

beauty with dark, flowing hair, a pair of haunted, deep green eyes, and a voice that could rage, roar, weep, or plead. She had over twenty quality feature pictures to her credit and commanded respect and admiration both within and outside the industry. She also received the top plaudit—she was bankable: If you had Melissa in your picture you could get financial backing for it.

The doorbell chimed and Melissa jumped. She waited for someone else to answer it before remembering she was the only one there. It had to be the TV repairman. She walked down the Spanish tile entranceway to the front of the house and swung open the solid oak door.

Two men pushed past her into the house with a suddenness that surprised and startled her. She had no lines ready for them, and she stood there too shocked to say a word.

"Miss Martindale?" one of the pair of six-footers said. He was the thinner one, with black hair and a moustache. Both wore cheap suits that looked as if they needed another wardrobe fitting.

"Why, yes, I'm Melissa Martindale. You must be the TV repairman."

"Hell no," the thinner one said. He turned toward the living room.

"Then get out of my house! You certainly shouldn't be here." She stood there holding the front door open and felt foolish as the two men strode into the living room. It was a poorly thought out scene from a half-rehearsed first act, she thought as she ran after them. What on earth did they think they were doing?

They stood in her beautifully furnished, forty-foot-long living room staring around. Oil paintings hung on the walls, gold-framed mirrors added an elegant touch, and the whole room was decorated in the fashionable style of the 1800s. She'd spent a fortune on that room alone.

"Gentlemen, I must insist that you leave my house. I don't want you here. You got in by deception, and you must leave now." It sounded like a line right out of *The Unsuspecting Bride,* only this time she gave it more feeling.

The dark-haired man, who spoke before, looked at her and laughed. He pointed to a two-by-three-foot oil portrait of Melissa.

"Hey, that picture is of you!" he said.

She nodded. "Yes, now please leave, or I'll have to call the guard."

"Lady, you ain't got no guard, and your maid is off, and your manager is at Universal, and your cook had two flat tires. So don't try to bullshit us." The man walked to the portrait, took a knife, and Melissa heard the terrible ripping, slicing sound as the sharp blade made a dozen long cuts in the portrait, ruining it forever.

"Oh, no! No, you can't do that!" She ran at the large man, crashed into him, and bounced off. He never budged. She staggered backward in amazement. He was like a block wall. He turned and pushed her farther away.

"Feisty little bitch, ain't you?"

Her mind was lurching crazily. Who were they? Why were they here? She would have them arrested! Yes. Identify them, prove that they were here! She ran to an antique secretary on the far wall and took out her camera. She had become quite good with it and had taken a great many pictures on her sets. Now she focused on the men and began snapping pictures. One looked up and saw her.

"Hey, dumb-dumb, no pictures. Hey, she wants to

take our pictures; ain't that nice." In three long strides, the blond reached her, grabbed the camera with one meaty hand, and tore it from her grasp. The force of his motion strained her shoulder, and she cried out.

"Now let me take some shots of you, big-assed movie star." The blondish man said it with a smile. He pretended to take one picture after another, then dropped the camera. It bounced on the rug without showing any damage. He took the camera to the fireplace and dropped it again, this time on the thick slate covering the raised hearth. The lens cracked.

Melissa cried out in alarm. "No, that's my favorite camera!"

"Tough," the blond man said. He opened the Nikon, ripped out the film, and unwound it from the spool, totally ruining any pictures that might have been there. He threw the camera and the worthless film in the fireplace.

On the mantle rested a sculptured marble head of Melissa. It had been commissioned and done nearly five years ago and cost over forty thousand dollars. Critics said it was modeled at the height of Melissa's physical beauty. She was prouder of the sculpture than of some of her movies. The great Donaldo of Italy had done it, and that made the work even more special to her.

The blond man scooped the Florentine marble sculpture off its stand and held it a moment. Then he dropped it on the slate. The nose broke off.

"Oh, no!" Melissa screamed and slumped in a chair. She was afraid she was going to faint. "Oh, no, not my sculpture. I'll pay you anything—just don't drop it." It wasn't movie dialogue now. Melissa had never felt so alone, so frightened, so threatened, in her life. Yet neither of the men had harmed her.

9

He threw the head down again, cracking the slate, tearing an ear and part of the flowing hair off the marble. The third time he threw the sculptured head against the slate, a quarter of it split off and he was satisfied.

"That's enough for now," he said to the dark-haired man. "We can always come back, anytime!" He sat down in a chair across from Melissa.

"Well, well, well. Ms. Martindale, the movie star. Very important lady in this movie town. That's why our mutual friend would be more than pleased if you would sign the contract he sent you for agent representation. In case you lost it, I have a duplicate copy for your signature."

She stood, her head whirling, but more angry now than frightened.

"Look, you cheap son of a bitch. Now I know why you're here. You're two goons trying to terrorize me into signing. You break in here, ruin my art, slash my portrait, break up my sculpture. You're trying to force me to sign that rotten contract. That's not the way to pressure me, buster!" She stalked the length of the room, her hands on her hips. Melissa couldn't remember ever being so angry at anyone. She stopped in front of the blond and kicked him in the shinbone. She knew it hurt, but he never flinched.

"You can tell your hoodlum boss that I'm not signing with him, that I'll never sign, that I'd rather starve than put my name on his contract. Take that back to your boss. Now get the hell out of my house!"

"Don't get so excited," the man said. "It's just a simple business deal and I bet we can negotiate. We got all day."

Melissa ran for the end of the room, picked up the phone, and dialed O for operator. Before the voice came on the line, one of the men jerked the phone from her hands and he pushed her to the floor.

"Sorry we have to get a little rough with you, Melissa Martindale. Personally I like your acting, but they tell me I ain't got good taste." He stared down at her. "As I remember, you're right handed."

Tears started to come. She nodded. The blond knelt beside her and helped her sit up. Then he took her left arm, held it at her wrist and elbow, and brought it down sharply across his knee. Both bones broke like sticks of kindling.

Melissa remembered hearing the bones snap, and seeing the look of satisfaction on the man's face. Her scream came at once, ending in a blubbering sound as she passed out and slid down to the forty-two-dollar-per-square-yard golden harvest carpet.

Two days later, a small item appeared in Hollywood's daily *Variety*, the movie business trade paper. It said that Melissa Martindale had joined a growing number of important stars who had signed a long-term contract with Global Talent Associates for agent representation, publicity, and personal management.

Brad Russell continued his workout in his private, at-home gym as the visitor came in. His doorman, butler-cook, and handyman, Lin Yee, showed her into the room, nodded to Russell, and withdrew. Brad counted two more pushups to make an even fifty, then sat on the rug. He toweled off his face and head, turned and looked at her, and grinned.

"You're back. Those folks sure do know how to go about trying to make a sale, sweetheart, but like I say, I'm happy with things the way they are, and I don't plan on making any changes."

The visitor was a girl, long blond hair with a

Fawcett cut, high, full breasts surging against a stark white blouse that had one button too many left open.

She walked over to Brad, knelt beside him, and twirled the brown hair on his chest.

"When they say you're all man, I see what they mean!" She looked pointedly down at the bulge in the tight shorts Brad wore. Then she sniffed. "Hey, I really do love that heavy-man smell when you perspire that way. It turns me on like crazy."

"That's about all the turn-on you're getting around here, sweetheart. I told them, and I told you last week, and I'm telling you again. I like my agent; I've been with him a long time, and I'm staying with him. No deal."

She unbuttoned the blouse, and her breasts surged out, swinging freely. She laughed. "Oops! I opened one button too many!"

Brad stood. "Little girl. Put your big tits away and go home. You haven't got anything I want. You should know that I don't go for the big silicone boobs."

She jumped up and tried to kick him in the crotch. He lifted his knee in defense and swatted her on her tight rump.

"Like I said, sweetheart, get your ass out of here before I bring in Lin Yee. Now he's a real tit freak, and he'll give you a Chinese bang you'll never forget. Move it!"

Brad watched her button her blouse, then ushered her down to the front door.

"Sure you don't want a friendly little pop? What would it hurt?"

"Me. Now vamoose!"

She paraded to the car, wiggling everything she had, and spun the wheels on her Le Car as she went down his drive. Brad laughed. Some of them just never gave up trying.

About ten o'clock that evening Brad brought his date back to her Hollywood Hills apartment. He parked the Rolls Royce and looked over at Jan, a small bundle of brunette who made him turn cartwheels.

"A drink and a few records?" he asked.

"Why not?"

He left the Rolls, closed the door carefully, and headed around the back of the car. Someone across the street called him by name. He turned, squinting into the light, and realized he'd fallen into the oldest trap in the world. He looked back towards the near curb just in time to see a blurred shape before something came down on his head. He sighed softly and crumpled.

When Brad returned to consciousness, he realized he was tied hand and foot and in the backseat of his own car. It was moving, and he heard voices in the front seat. Neither voice was Jan Sinclair's, the tiny brunette. They were the voices of two men. The car kept moving for twenty minutes before it stopped, and the driver got out, leaving the engine running.

A moment later they pulled Brad out of the backseat and stood him up. They were on a road, out of town. He recognized the area, Mulholland Drive, the curving, twisting mountain road high in the Hollywood Hills. He saw Jan in the car, her head back against the seat, eyes closed. Someone took the cord off her hands and her ankles, and he was sure she was unconscious. He tried to see faces, but the two men holding him wore masks. A hand shifted the car into gear, and it began rolling forward. Someone ran alongside the driver's window, steering the car. His Rolls was headed for the

13

edge of the road—it was near a dropoff and there was no guardrail!

"Stop the car! Stop it—you'll kill her!" Brad shouted.

Both men ignored him. The runner kept up with the car, steering it, pushing. Suddenly the front wheel lurched off the side of the road, the frame scraped on gravel for a moment, and the rear tires spun slightly as the Rolls went hurtling forward and was airborne. The car fell out of sight.

"My God, you've killed her!" Brad screamed. An arm moved and a lead kosh hit his head again, precisely, expertly, and Brad Russell, movie tough guy, sagged helpless into a tall blond man's arms.

Later, Brad felt consciousness returning. It was a soupy, listless feeling followed by pain and fuzzy eyes. Slowly he blinked the fog away. It wasn't a bad dream, a ruthless nightmare—it was real! Dark. Yes, it all was dark. He tried to move, but could not. Tied up, trapped somewhere? No, he was more wedged in than trapped. Why couldn't he see something? His hands probed, and he felt the familiar wheel, the steering wheel. His Rolls Royce. He was back inside his Rolls! They must have carried him down the cliff while he was unconscious and stuffed him inside the car. Why?

Voices. He heard voices and saw a light far above. Were they on top of the cliff? The car lay on its side. The driver's crushed door aimed at the sky. He tried again but still couldn't move. Something pressed down against him. Curiously, he didn't seem hurt. Nothing ached but his head, which split into a dozen pieces. He had been knocked unconscious twice tonight. His doctor would have a fit.

My God, why had someone done this to him? Jan? How far was the drop? He tried to turn his head to

14

look down where she must be, but he couldn't move that far. He could see only one of her hands. It stretched up towards him as if she were trying to reach him. That's all he could make out in the darkness. Something had smashed through the windshield and separated them. A big rock? He wasn't sure.

They deliberately ran the car over the cliff, with Jan inside. That's murder. He was lucky to be alive. No, they wanted him alive. Why? They took him out, and they put him back inside for the police to find. The cops would never believe him. What if they planted cocaine in the wreckage? If they hurt Jan, he would make sure the cops believed him! Hell, no, he'd find whoever did this and strangle them to death!

The light worked closer. He could hear voices again, and they were louder. Should he call out? No, they wouldn't hear yet. The closer the lights came, the weaker he felt. He couldn't understand it. He didn't hurt; he guessed he wasn't even bleeding. Why should he feel so weak? Shock. Hell, yes, shock. He'd done enough doctor movies to know that. Closer, hang on a few minutes more. Just before the rescue squad reached the wrecked Rolls Royce, Brad Russell passed out again.

It took the police and firemen fifteen minutes to pry and cut Brad out of the wrecked Rolls. Now he sat in an ambulance letting the paramedic check him over. The medic couldn't find anything wrong with him either but was instructed to bring him into the hospital anyway.

Brad had two blankets wrapped around him and still felt cold. He had a small scratch on his cheek. The paramedic shook his head.

"Mr. Russell, there's no way you should even be alive after that wreck. You've got no broken bones, no internal injuries I can find. And your pulse is almost normal. Sure they didn't do that for some movie? You know, stunt men or something?"

"I wish my double had done it." Brad shivered. "So it's just shock, right?"

"Yeah, Brad. Just shock, but shock can kill you, too. Now lie down, and we'll get moving."

"Jan. They haven't told me about Jan. How is she?"

The paramedic looked away. "Oh, that's the other team's job. I was too busy taking care of you. That's my first job. Okay, Willy, let her roll."

That was when Brad knew. Jan was dead. There hadn't been any rush to get her out of the car. They worked on him first. He should have realized it right away. He knew it was true. She was dead, and that blond son of a bitch was to blame. The muscle men from Global Talent. He would never sign with them, not even if they killed him.

The day following his release from the hospital and after his miraculous escape from the death plunge of his Rolls Royce on Mulholland Drive in which his companion died, Brad Russell signed a contract with Global Talent Associates for representation and personal management.

Jerry Anderson was a top investigative reporter for the *Los Angeles Times*. He called his own shots, working as long as he needed to on a big story. All he had to do was convince his city editor that it was a worthwhile story, one that had a public interest involvement, and something the *Times* felt was important enough. He had done that with two quick interviews and had spent two more weeks digging up the guts of the story. He could get into offices, through doors, and talk to famous people in this town who would reveal facts to him that no one else could get.

People trusted Jerry Anderson. He always protected his news sources, and he never printed a word without checking it six ways to Sunday.

Now he backed his TR-7 out of the *Times'* parking garage and crawled through traffic toward the Hollywood Freeway heading for the Valley. He was still excited about his current story. Partly because the first of the six installments came out that morning. He had taken direct aim at Global Talent Associates, laying the groundwork for a series of accusations that could very well turn into indictments by the district attorney. The firm was putting illegal and highly questionable pressure on actors and actresses to sign heavy-handed, long-term contracts with Global. Jerry had names, dates, and medical records, more than enough to make the DA take a long, hard look at the agency.

He enjoyed his job, and a Jerry Anderson story had never been challenged in the courts through a lawsuit of any kind. He didn't use a story if there were any chance that it might be wrong or that some of his key witnesses were going to bomb out on him.

That was one thing nobody could take away from him. When a Jerry Anderson story came out, everyone could believe it.

Under the hood of the TR-7 near the fourth cylinder, fastened securely to the engine head, rested a thermo-couple. It monitored the heat of the engine as the temperature gradually rose from the ambient Los Angeles iron mass norm of about eighty-eight degrees.

Just as Jerry Anderson turned north on Hollywood Boulevard, the thermo-couple activated, sending a small electric current that turned on a delicate timer.

Firmly taped against the metal directly under the

17

driver's seat lay a package of ten sticks of sixty-percent dynamite. The timer had been set for four minutes and was attached to a pencil-type detonator inserted into one of the dynamite sticks. Precisely four minutes after the thermo-couple activated, the detonator went off, triggering the explosion of the dynamite.

The TR-7 suddenly reared upwards, four feet over the traffic lane. The initial force blew the driver's seat, passenger, and roof section 500 feet into the air, shattering the metal, shredding the physical remains of Jerry Anderson into thousands of pieces, and dropping flesh, bone, wire, metal, and upholstery over a block-wide radius. The car came apart at the welds; the four wheels and tires sheared off and went rolling down the freeway. The largest piece of the car left was the twisted, mangled form of the frame and body and what was left of the engine.

The intensity of the ten-stick explosion immediately shattered the TR-7's nearly full gas tank, spilling the flaming gasoline into the very heart of the explosive cauldron, a millisecond after the eruption, and adding a secondary blast as the vaporized gasoline burned at the speed of 2,200 feet per second. The now blackened and burned hulk of the TR-7 lay three hundred feet farther up the freeway and on the other side of the divider fence from the scorch marks on the paving that marked the spot of the first detonation.

Seven other cars smashed into the debris, skidded, and crashed, or drivers panicked when the blast took place and lost control of their vehicles. Three deaths were reported in the tragedy on Los Angeles' six o'clock news broadcasts.

Chapter 2

FINDING A TARGET

Mark Hardin pinched dripping perspiration from his nose and took a dozen deep breaths, toweled himself off, and drank sixteen ounces of lukewarm Quick Kick as he scanned the bulletin board. He was just back from a ten-mile conditioning run through the Calico mountain desert near Barstow, California. The next day he would go twenty miles.

Now he could relax and look over the Alert Board in the communications room at the Stronghold. He was in the nerve center of his fight against crime—and an important part of Dr. Willard Haskins' camouflaged hideout built into the upper levels of an old borax mine not too far from Barstow.

The communications room had the UPI newswire, a special law enforcement agency teletype that they had rigged with the cooperation of Captain Kelly Patterson in the Los Angeles sheriff's office. The captain was one of Mark's few friends among law enforcement men and had worked with him on the Penetrator's very first strike.

There were radios, the audio-fence alert system around the Stronghold and its visual display board, the

19

computer, readout and printout systems, long- and short-wave radio and two telephone lines that the phone people thought were simply local lines in Riverside.

The Alert Board was an eight-foot-long and four-foot-wide bulletin board with position numbers from one to ten. Under many of the numbers were reports, clips from newspapers, telex strips, notes, and messages. The ten numbers represented the ten most important problems that were potential assignments for the Penetrator. The board was updated each day, and gradually some items worked towards the top while others faded and were replaced.

Now Mark stared at a picture of movie star Melissa Martindale and the story about her signing with GTA. Under it was a story about Brad Russell and his miraculous escape from a car wreck with a notice two days later about his signing with GTA. The initials struck a responsive chord in the Penetrator.

A week after he returned from New York and his brief vacation with Lennie Gorse, he had telephoned her friend in Hollywood, who said some wild and weird things were going on in tinsel town. She had been all excited about GTA, Global Talent Agency, and said they were gobbling up as much talent as they could get. She had heard that they had been threatening some people. Mark made a note about it, gave her Lennie's regards, and thought little more about it.

Now he kept seeing GTA show up in more and more places. In the strip of telex and news wire he found an item about Melissa Martindale breaking her left arm in a fall at home. It had not held up the made-for-TV movie she was working on. They simply wrote the fall into the script, and she appeared in the rest of the film with her broken arm in a cast. Mark checked the dates. The GTA signing had been announced two days after she reportedly broke her arm at home.

Mark shook his head. Strong-arm tactics by a talent agency against stars like Melissa and Brad? It was unheard of, unthinkable. He moved to another room, picked up a phone, and called a name he had heard about in Hollywood, one of the top five talent agencies in the business. The phone rang twice, and a faintly English-accented voice came on.

"Good morning, Global Talent Agency. May I help you?"

"Global? I was looking for Mendenhal Talent."

"Yes, sir, same number. Mendenhal Talent merged with GTA about six months ago. We serve most of their old clients. What can we do for you?"

"Oh, it isn't that. I'm hunting Bob Mendenhal. A personal friend. Is he still with the agency?"

"No. Mr. Mendenhal sold out and now is in some other line of work. I don't have his new number."

"Yes, okay, and thanks." Mark hung up. It was the same phone line Ma Bell thought ended in Riverside. The bill was sent to a blind drop in Riverside and forwarded monthly to Chicago, where it was picked up by air freight and returned to the Riverside airport. David Red Eagle picked up the packet once a month. It was impossible to trace back ownership of the number to the Stronghold or to the Penetrator.

Mark frowned and slapped the desk top. Somehow he couldn't imagine Bob Mendenhal doing anything else but talent agency work. It had been his whole life. But evidently he was gone from the business.

Mark headed for a shower. He knew he should go down to the sweat lodge Red Eagle had built deep below, but he felt a touch of urgency now. He showered

21

quickly, dressed, and went back to the telephone. The Penetrator was trying to piece together a half-remembered name from the past. One of his fraternity brothers had become a talent agent. The kid had tried to be an actor, but didn't make it that way. Then Mark remembered the name, Joey Larson. The Los Angeles yellow pages coughed up the same name, Joey Larson Talent Agency. Mark dialed it direct and waited. The phone rang seven times.

"Yeah, good morning, Joey Larson Talent. We've got just the talent you need."

"Hi, Joey. You probably don't remember me. I'm Mark Hardin from UCLA."

"Hell, yes, man, I remember you! We were in the same frat house, and you were a jock and a year ahead of me. How the hell is it going, buddy?"

"Fine. What I'm wondering is how things are with you? You still in the talent agent business?"

"You bet, and going great. Couldn't be better. Where are you now?"

"Near L.A. What I'd really like to do is ask if you know anything about an outfit called the Global Talent Agency."

There was a long pause.

"GTA? Mark, I don't understand. You're not in this business. How did you even hear about them?"

"A friend of mine from New York said there were some strange things going on in the business. Then I heard about Melissa's broken wrist. I'm interested."

"You won't have any trouble finding out about GTA. Everybody in town knows about them. Nobody knew they existed a year ago. Hell, yes, I know about GTA. They're trying to steal my only good client. These guys really know how to put on the pressure. They go after an actor, and they get him. I've seen it happening for six, eight months now. I won't give them the time of day, but I don't know how long I can hold out against them. Already they fire bombed my office. I slept there that night and smothered the damn thing with my sleeping bag. Now I'm starting to get a little worried."

"You heard about that reporter for the *Los Angeles Times?*"

"Oh, yeah. Right. I heard about him. So did everyone else, and the story he was writing about GTA. Nothing was ever printed after that first part. Did you know that? The rest of the series of ten were lost. All of his notes and files mysteriously vanished right from his desk in the middle of the *Times* newsroom. Can you feature that? Oh, damn right, I've heard about Jerry Anderson."

"Joey, when can I come in and see you? Sounds like you need a friend about now. At least we can talk about it. I might be there when you need some help. I've handled a few rough boys in my time."

"No way, Mark. I'm not putting anybody's neck on the line but mine. I'm keeping that contract no matter what they do. But I've got to do this strictly on my own. You know what I mean, old buddy?"

"Yeah, Joey, I know. But at least we can talk. I want to know everything about GTA that you know. You might say I'm gathering material on them for a story of my own. Let's make it this afternoon. Anytime after lunch. What do you say?"

They met at four o'clock at Don Jose's, an excellent Mexican restaurant with waiters. Mark always felt self-conscious in any place that was so high class they had men serving the food.

Mark was surprised at Joey's appearance. He had

23

changed a lot in the decade since UCLA. Now he was half-bald, with glasses, fringes of black hair around the sides, a suit that needed a good pressing, and shoes that hadn't been polished in weeks.

He saw Mark coming and ran to greet him. Joey had been the house character, the cutup, always good for a laugh. He wasn't laughing now. They shook hands, slapped each other on the back, and went into the bar for margaritas. No other drink would do in Jose's, Joey said. They sat at the end of the bar, and Joey turned toward Mark so his back was to the wall. He sipped from the salt-rimmed glass and checked out everyone who came into the bar. Joey's hands didn't shake, but there was a nervous tic bothering one eye, and his glance darted to meet every new man or woman who came in. He couldn't relax. Mark knew the symptoms; Joey was scared to death.

They talked about the football games, the annual Gamma stag party, and whoopee night.

On the second margarita they got around to show biz.

"How many clients do you have under contract, Joey?"

"Seven. Exactly seven and most of them are losers. But I've got Randy Smith, and he's ready to break into the big time. That boy has so much talent it oozes out of him. He's had two starring roles in TV, and he's got a movie coming up. If I can just hold on until the flick is released, he'll be a real star, and I'll have my meal ticket." His enthusiasm faded, and he pulled on the drink.

"The only question is can I hang on and make it?" He waved a long, thin cigar he had lit a few minutes before. "Hell, yes. I realize that sounds a little bizarre.

24

But I've been in this damn town long enough to know what's going on. Things are getting rough."

"Joey, did GTA break Melissa Martindale's arm?"

Joey drained the last of the second margarita. He shivered.

"See what I mean? You figured that out, and you ain't been in town half an hour. Of course their goons broke her arm, and then a couple of days later she signs on the dotted line with GTA."

"Brad Russell?"

"Oh, cute. They treated him real cute. Remember how the police said it was a miracle that Brad wasn't killed in the wreck? No damn miracle. He just wasn't inside the car when they pushed it over the damn cliff. They stuffed him inside later." Joey signaled for another drink. "They won't be no way so fancy with me. I'm not a star. I'm just a little clod in their way. One of them big road rollers, the blacktop kind? That's what they'll use on me."

"Background, Joey, give me some facts. Who are they? Where did they come from? How did they get started? How do they operate?"

Joey bent over his fresh drink, and spoke low so only Mark could hear as he laid it all out. The firm was only a year old. It began by buying out four of the best talent agencies in town, thereby picking up a big stable of top stars. The price for each of the firms was at least fifty percent more than it was worth on the market. GTA bought them at a loss to corner the market on talent.

"Then they went after the smaller agencies, anyone with a rated star. When an agency wouldn't sell, they contacted the stars directly and found a way to break the contract. Then some of the smaller featured players moved to get on the GTA bandwagon, and the outfit

25

was rolling so fast nobody could stop it. Now the first spot a new actor hits is GTA to see if he can get taken on.

"In my case I have Randy Smith, and the word is out that he's a comer. I got a phone call with an offer, and they said a letter with a check in it would follow. It came the next day. A check for twenty thousand dollars. And it would have been all mnie! I haven't seen that kind of commission since I started the agency. On the back of the check were the conditions. I would sell them Randy's contract and not engage in the talent agency business in this area for movies or TV for a period of five years. I tore up the check and sent it back to them."

"Then the real harassment began?"

"Oh, yeah, the next day. Some hit-and-run driver creamed the whole side of my Pontiac. In Hollywood you don't drive around to important meetings with a lousy suit, a battered car, or bad breath, and now I had all three."

Joey stopped talking suddenly. The rest of the color drained from his face. He watched someone at the door. Mark looked in the bar mirror and saw a tall man standing in the doorway. He had on a suit that looked uncomfortable and a wind-blown crop of blond hair. His face was angry and searching.

"Jesus!" Joey said softly. "Their number-one goon. Suddenly I'm not so hungry anymore." Joey turned toward the bar, remembered the mirror, and edged around until his back was toward the man at the door.

Mark watched the blond man over the rim of his margarita glass through the mirror. He seemed to be looking over everyone in the bar. His eyes lingered on Joey's back and moved on. At last he twisted the side of his mouth in frustration and went into the restaurant.

"Is he gone?" Joey asked.

"Went into the main room."

"Then let's get the hell out of here!"

Mark threw some bills on the bar, and they slid off the stools and went out the side door. Joey breathed more easily.

"See that Pontiac over there with the side mashed in? That's mine. Let me check it out, and if it's clear, I'll drive over here and pick you up."

"They'll be watching your car, won't they?" Mark asked.

"Damn. Yeah, probably. But who cares? I might as well get it over with. I'm tired of being afraid all the time. Maybe if I get in my car, I can run over the son of a bitch."

Joey hurried for his car, unlocked the door, and was about to get in when a man stepped from behind a van. Mark saw the gun in the stranger's hand.

"Look out, Joey!" Mark shouted.

Joey dropped beside his car out of sight. The man with the gun whirled toward Mark's voice but couldn't locate him. Then the gunman too bent low so Mark couldn't see him. Mark sprinted for the spot he had last seen the gunman. Two cars drove into the lot. Three couples came out of the restaurant, and a moment later the lot was full of people getting in and out of cars. Mark had no idea where the man with the gun was or which one he was. Two men alone walked away from the area, and Mark wondered if one were the gunman. He couldn't tell. He went to Joey's car, got in, and they drove out of the parking lot, down Sunset a dozen blocks, turned off the mainstem, and stopped beside the curb.

27

"Who was that back there?" Joey asked.

"A man with a gun. I didn't get a good look at him, but it was a small pistol of some kind, and it had a silencer on the end. Somebody meant business."

Joey slumped in the seat. "I'm just a small business-man. Who is this who's after me, the goddamned Mafia?"

"I don't think so, Joey. They wouldn't have missed or been so obvious. No, it's not the Cosa Nostra."

"Who else could be behind the GTA?"

"Joey, I don't know, but you stay alive the next week or so, and I'm going to find out."

"Mark, I can't let you get involved with this. These guys play rough."

"Yes, rough, but in an amateur sort of way. I can get a little unpleasant myself. I put in some time in Nam, remember? Now I suggest you forget about going home or to your office for a week or so. Just let things slide, and stay out of sight. Let them look for you. Rent a motel room somewhere, sleep a lot, and watch television. Give me the name of a motel right now, so I'll have a contact with you. I've got to find out a lot more about this GTA outfit."

Chapter 3

THE INSIDE STORY

Before Mark left Joey that afternoon, he had the agent registered and settled down at the Capri Motel. Mark told him he'd call the next day and see how he was getting along. He emphasized again that Joey should not go near his office or apartment.

Two blocks from the motel, Mark pulled up to a phone booth and called the Stronghold, where he talked to Professor Haskins. Mark explained what he needed, and the professor said it wouldn't be any big problem. Part of the package would be ready before Mark got back to the Stronghold that evening.

At nine-thirty the following morning, Mark walked into the GTA general offices on Sunset Boulevard. His casual suit, worn without a tie, was neat, conservative, and expensive. Under his arm was a portfolio of pictures and clippings concerning Lance Lansing, actor.

The small brunette at the reception desk eyed him with cool detachment, and Mark realized that she must see most of the biggest stars of Hollywood and TV parade past her desk. He stopped in front of her and put on his best smile.

"My name is Lance Lansing, and I'd like to talk to someone about having GTA represent me."

She glanced up with a tentative, uncertain look that gave Mark the idea she wasn't sure who he was or if she should know him.

"Do you have an appointment, Mr. Lansing?"

"No, I called yesterday, and the lady told me I wouldn't need one. She said just to come down with my material and see you." Mark tried to grin a break through her reserve, and her face relaxed a little.

"Why don't you sit down over there, Mr. Lansing, and I'll try to get you in to see Ms. Harriet Bartholemew. She's one of our best talent evaluators."

Mark said he would and went to sit where she pointed. The lobby was two stories tall, with a huge swirling cascading chandelier of cut glass sparkling and tinkling in the hushed movement of the air-conditioning. The carpet had double padding under it, and Mark thought he would sink up to his ankles. The soft-cushioned sofas around the lobby made it look more like a living room than an outer reception area. Mark settled down on the first unoccupied couch beside a small redhead who looked scared and sat on the very edge of the couch, her knees and feet set precisely together as she stared at the receptionist.

Mark could guess only that she was trying to use some kind of mind-over-matter power on the other girl to get in to see someone important.

Five minutes later a speaker hidden somewhere softly directed Mr. Lansing to come to room nine. The redhead gave Mark a scathing look as he got up. He asked the receptionist how he could find room nine, and she pointed him toward the right hallway.

There was nothing cheap about GTA. Behind the first door in the hall the carpet was just as thick, the oil

30

paintings on the wall a bit better in style and technique. He found room nine, turned the knob, and went in.

The room was done in early 1930s style, with pictures of England's little princesses on the wall, framed newspaper front pages from the depression days, and a series of two-by-three-foot stills from motion pictures honored as the best of the year. Three films were highlighted: *Free Soul* with a shot of Lionel Barrymore; a life-size cutout of Marie Dressler near a photograph of her in her role in *Min and Bill*; there were four scenes from the famous *Cimarron* western action film.

"Well, young man, do you approve of my interior decoration?"

She sat behind a small wooden desk, with a clean, polished top. The woman was in her forties, wore too much makeup to hide the wrinkles, but didn't seem to care. Her hair was bleached frankly blonde and set every morning to camouflage just how little of it was left.

"Sit down, young man. Lansing, isn't it? You've picked a famous name; I hope you can live up to it. Lance Lansing—yes, it has a good alliterative ring. I like that. Could I see your book and your portfolio?"

Mark nodded and opened the thirty-inch-square, sleek presentation folder of heavy plastic. Inside were mounted pictures showing Mark in a dozen different poses, all carefully photographed the night before in Barstow by a studio owner who had done work for the professor before. They were typical "studio glamour shots" and Mark had been surprised at how slick the layout was and how well they had all come out. The thick scrapbook was filled with printed reviews of Lance Lansing's extensive theatre experience, starting at UCLA and going through six seasons of summer stock, the Old Globe Theatre in San Diego, the West-

31

wood Theatre and the Huntington Hartford in the Los Angeles area. The reviews ranged from lukewarm to raves. He laid both showpieces on her desk and stood back, unconsciously reverting to the military parade rest position with his hands locked behind his back and his feet apart. He eased out of the pose before she noticed it.

"Please, Lance. Sit down. I hate it when an actor towers over me this way."

Mark sat in the upholstered chair at the side of her desk.

She checked the photos first and nodded. "Well, you certainly are photogenic. Those smoldering good looks of yours transfer to film remarkably well. Frankly, that surprises me. So many men simply look gorgeous in person and fade away on film. You look terrific both ways." She watched him a moment, caught his eye, smiled, and looked at his book. She scanned the items briefly before going on.

"You're looking for representation, right, Lance?"

"Yes."

"Why did you come to GTA? Don't you know we handle the biggest names in the business?"

"Sure, and mine will be right up there with them in two-and-a-half years."

She smiled. "Confidence. We like that here. But why do you give yourself such a short time?"

"My own deadline. I'll be thirty by then."

She laughed, and he knew she had been an actress herself.

"Ah, the glory, the impatience, the naivete of youth! Damn—I wish I had some of it back." She stood. "Come along, Lance. Bring your books. I want you to meet Johnathan Westerly. He's a bit on the crude side but really rather good. He has a sense about people, whether they will make it in this business or not. Don't ask me how he does it. You don't talk much, do you?"

"I've been known to ad-lib a few lines, Ms. Bartholemew. But I seldom put on an act unless I'm getting paid for it."

Her head snapped up, eyes stern, until she saw the smile brightening Mark's face, and she laughed. "Yes, that's good. I like that. A sense of humor, too, and in this business we all need that." She touched a button on her desk and pointed toward a wall.

"This way, Lance. It will be interesting to see how Johnathan reacts. She went to a paneled wall, pushed a concealed button, and a section slid back, opening into a reception office. She nodded at a girl behind a desk and walked past her to another door, which she opened, and they went in.

The office was thirty feet long and a dozen feet wide. It was startling, decorated in modern plush. The carpet was a foot deep in bright red and brown swirls. Upholstered furniture to seat twenty clustered the near end of the room, arranged around a low, self-service wet bar. At the far end of the room on a foot-high raised platform sat a desk. It didn't look large until you came to it. Then Mark saw that it was double a regular-sized executive desk and overflowing with papers, envelopes, scripts, pictures, portfolios and folders of every description.

The man behind the desk looked up from under heavy brows, his red hair a fuzzy, tightly curled permanent that looked like a honkey afro, and a pair of oversized glasses of the change-tint lens type. His mouth was thin and nervous, and now brown eyes glared at Ms. Bartholemew.

"Harriet, what the hell do you want?"

33

"Good morning, sunshine. I have a once-and-future star for you, darling. How do you like the package?"

Westerly stood and stared at Mark. He walked around Mark once, flopped in his chair, and sipped a tall drink without offering anything to the others.

"Yeah, Harriet, possible. But you're screening again with your goddamned crotch, not your head. We're talking about actors here, remember, not just some hunk of man as a playmate on your waterbed. Try to remember that."

"Johnathan, the thought never entered my mind . . ."

"It didn't have to. Since you think with your crotch, the idea was already down there. Let's see his mugs."

She handed the man the portfolio and stepped back.

Westerly gave a short sigh and shook his head. "All right, Harriet, get your crotch out of here. I'll be glad to take over from here." His voice had the snap of command, but the animosity came through clearly. Westerly simply hated her guts and didn't care who knew it, especially Harriet. She smiled valiantly, turned, and without a word went back through the door and closed it.

Westerly didn't notice. He was staring at the pictures on his desk. "Yeah, not bad. You come across good in photos. That surprises me, and usually I can tell." He opened the thick bio scrapbook and looked at the last and most recently dated pages. "Hartford, huh? You one of them fucking artistic actors, or can you do a job and bring it in on time?"

"I play it however the director wants me to. I'm good. I can play any kind of part, and I don't take any shit from anybody."

Westerly's eyes came up to meet Mark's. They stared at each other for a moment, and Westerly looked

34

away and laughed. "Yes, I can see that you don't. What kind of credits do you have? Any movies?"

"Just some bit parts shown there. I'm looking for a top agent to put me in business."

"And you're in your late twenties? You should have more credits by now."

"Army. I got drafted for two years."

"You're too young for that. Hell, it doesn't matter." He sat down and looked at the pictures again. "Okay, we'll take you on, but at twenty percent for representation and twenty percent for personal management and PR. Actually you might make it, but you're a big risk. You're too old for the big kid buildup, and you don't have enough solid credits for a man your age. You're in between. But for forty percent we'll take a chance."

Mark laughed, reached for his portfolio and book. "You're crazy. I wouldn't give you more than ten percent for this whole outfit. I've got my own PR and management. Besides, I don't like your looks." Mark grabbed his material, and Westerly held out his hand to stop him. Mark chopped down on the wrist to hurt him but not break any bones. Westerly howled and leaned back.

"Westerly, I don't know who the hell you think you are, but like I told you, I won't let anybody push me around. Especially not a son of a bitch like you with an asinine white-trash afro haircut. That's the most stupid-looking hair I've seen since the depression pictures."

Westerly jumped out of his chair, scowling at Mark.

"Get out of my office, you pimp! Move your ass, now!"

"Westerly, what is it about you that I just can't stomach? Is it your beady little brown eyes or those swindler-type lips you have? Hey, now I have it. It's that smell. All that damn shaving lotion and body oil and perfume. You smell like a two-dollar male whore waiting for his sweet little boyfriend pimp."

Westerly stood well behind his desk now, his eyes wide with surprise and anger. He waved a fisted hand at Mark. "What are you trying to do? Now get out of here. I warned you. I gave you a chance." He leaned to the desk and pressed a buzzer. Five seconds later two men came in from a door behind Westerly. One of them was over six feet tall with exprizefighter stamped all over his battered face. The second man was shorter, with a flat-top haircut. He was cleaning his fingernails with a four-inch switchblade knife.

They stopped just inside and closed the door. Like two well-trained dogs, they looked at their master.

"Boys, glad you could stop by," Westerly said. "This slob is due for a treatment. Take him down the backstairs, and mess up his face a little. Don't break anything on purpose, but make him so sore he won't sleep for a week."

The two enforcers said nothing. They split and came toward Mark from opposite sides. Mark watched them, evaluating the pair, deciding they were no dangerous threat. He'd go for the one with the knife first.

Mark laid down his pictures and clippings, turned toward the big man, at once changed directions, and —in a classic drop kick—jumped at the goon with the knife. His polished shoe caught the knife hand before the attacker could move it, jolting the blade away just as Mark's left foot slammed flat into the surprised man's chest, driving him backwards and to the floor.

Mark dropped to the soft carpet on his hands and feet, came upright at once, and sidestepped the tall man's rush. The trip didn't work. The big man turned

36

and came back, his hands out in a wrestler's pose. Mark faked a kick at his crotch, pulled back as the man turned, and went in over the distracted right hand with a sweeping karate chop at the man's neck. The blow jolted the expug, and Mark spun him, wrapped his arm around the man's neck, and applied a police "sleeper" hold.

His wrist and arm pressed in on both sides of the man's neck where the carotid arteries send blood to the brain. Mark lifted the man partly off his feet, bending him backward to apply more pressure on the arteries.

The only drawback to the sleeper hold is that it takes fifteen to twenty seconds to work. The blood supply is shut off to the subject's brain, and he drops into unconsciousness. There is some danger from the hold, but police departments in almost every town in the nation use it. They say it's less dangerous than other methods of subduing violent persons.

Mark watched the small knife wielder. He was crawling around on the floor looking for his blade. The exfighter collapsed, and Mark released the hold and dropped him on the carpet. In two strides Mark stood over the knifeman.

"You really don't want to get up, do you dumb-dumb?"

The man looked at Mark, his hand a foot from the knife. He stared at his buddy, then at Mark's foot poised to lash out at him again. For just a second he glanced at his boss, who had frozen in his chair. The knife wielder slowly shook his head to answer Mark's question.

"Then down on the floor, on your belly, hands and feet spread." Mark snapped the order like a cop, and the man flattened out on the floor away from the knife. Mark turned and walked to Westerly's desk.

37

"You're next, big shot. I'm going to break half the bones in your body just for practice."

Westerly stared at him; then his eyes rolled up, and his head sagged to his chest. He had fainted. Mark snorted. The rough, tough Westerly with the big mouth was a chicken at heart.

Mark slipped a riot cuff from his pocket. It was a strip of plastic a half-inch wide and eight inches long with a slit in one end. Mark put it around Westerly's crossed wrists and inserted the end through the slot. He cinched it up tight. Barbs on the sides of the plastic prevented it from being loosened. It had to be cut off.

Mark took a two-inch-long flint arrowhead from his pocket. It was a Cheyenne-chipped blue flint, an authentic, recently made arrowhead. He laid it on Westerly's desk, picked up his portfolio and scrapbook, and vanished out the side door the two enforcers had used. He was in a hall that led to the rear entrance. A moment later Mark was on the street and walking back to his car. His first soft entry into the GTA stronghold was completed. But he would be back later, after it was dark when there would be no one around to interrupt his search.

Chapter 4

LOVELY LORNA LUNA

Just after lunch Mark called Joey at his hideout motel.
The agent was still there but getting anxious.

"Hey, I'm not doing anyone any good lying around
here," Joey said as soon as Mark said hello. "I should
be out there earning some money or at least giving
GTA a bad time."

"You're staying alive, Larson; that's doing one hell
of a lot. Now just relax, take a nap, watch some football or some game shows. But first I want a list of
some of the top stars who are now represented by
GTA. Some you remember besides Melissa and Brad."

"That's easy. How many do you need? One of the
biggest is Lorna Luna, a can-do-any-part star. She's
evidently signed on or was picked up quickly. Then
there's Alice and Farrah, Travolta, Hemingway, Hope,
Allen, Sommers, Lawrence, Burnett, Peck, Bujold,
Asner . . . how much longer do you want me to keep
talking?"

"Lorna? Lorna Luft?"

"No, Lorna Luna, a smash back in the late fifties,
and she's been on top ever since. She just finished *The
Long Night* that's being released now."

"Right, I've got some names. Now can you make

39

some phone calls and get me in to see some of these people?"

"One of them for sure. Melissa is at Universal on a TV flick. I can get you past the gates there. I think she's on sound stage fourteen. Check with anyone after you're inside."

Mark told him about his interview that morning at GTA on Sunset.

"Sounds like you have all the fun. Why don't you use that Lance Lansing name out at Universal and see if anyone jumps?"

"Fine. Now what about Brad Russell? I'd like to get his side of the wreck story."

"I'm not much help there. I don't know his home address or private phone number. But I do know when he's not working he usually takes a run around the UCLA campus and track. You might catch him there in the afternoon."

"So far, great. What about the other one, Lorna Luna?"

"Easy. Everyone knows where she lives. She's on all the stars' homes maps. It's 2323 Ladyflower Lane in Beverly Hills. But that's about all the good I can do for you there. I can't get you in to see her."

"No sweat, I'll find a way. You've done more than enough. Now stick close to that room, and get your meals sent in if you want to. I'll pick up the tab, so don't worry about that. No sense taking any chances for the next few days."

They said goodbye, and Mark drove to Universal Studios out the Hollywood Freeway at the edge of the Valley. He parked in the visitors' lot and used the name Joey had given him with the guard.

"I have an appointment with Jerry Whitehaven," Mark said.

40

"Just a moment, sir," the guard said and made a phone call. He hung up and gave Mark a visitor's badge. "Mr. Whitehaven said for you to come right in." He pointed out the general direction for Mark to go to find Whitehaven's office.

Once inside the lot Mark walked around purposefully for a few minutes to get the lay of the land before he went toward sound stage fourteen. The big door was open so he walked in. He found a maze of lights, cables, false front sets, and, at the far end, a lighted set with people around it.

Mark walked that way and heard an assistant director call out sharply.

"All right, people, we're trying to make a picture here. Let's have it quiet on the set for a rehearsal." The set hushed at once. Someone called "action" and two people walked through doors that led to an outside street scene where the two bumped into each other sending packages scattering into the pretend snow on the sidewalk. The man looked surprised, jumped to help the woman, and did a pratfall, grinning sheepishly.

"Cut. Hold it, Jerry. Jer. Jer, baby. I told you you've got to have the fall pads in your pants, or it's going to be obvious that you're anticipating the fall, and it won't look natural. We'll cut around your padded butt when we do the scene and then edit in some nice, smooth rear end shots for your fans. Let's try it once more, and this time, Jer, put in the goddamned pads, preferably on the backside."

There was a lull while they waited for the costume changes. On one side Mark saw a woman with several people hovering around her. He recognized her as Melissa Martindale, and he knew for sure when he saw her left arm in a sling and a cast. Mark worked that direction. He edged in and soon was standing beside the star.

At a pause in the conversation he caught her eye. "Melissa, I loved your work in *The Misapprehension,* some beautiful bits."

"Thank you. It was a dream part."

"Sorry about your arm, but they wrote it into the script, didn't they? Was there much reshooting?"

"Only two scenes, which was no problem."

Mark smiled and stared at her. "Melissa, is it true that two men from GTA broke your arm?"

Her eyes flared wide open for a moment, then closed to normal, and her famous lips parted. For a second she smiled. "I don't know who you are, but if you're from one of those scandal magazines, I'm not even talking to you. I certainly have no idea what you're saying. I broke my arm in a fall at my home. Now if you'll excuse me, I have to get back to work."

Mark watched her walk away. She was cool, her emotions absolutely controlled after the first shock of the idea that someone knew or suspected. But she shut down the surprise and went back to her business of acting. Her whole routine here was an act. He knew she wouldn't tell him anything more about her arm. Mark got the idea she wouldn't say a word about it in private or public. He watched her walk onto the set and take the place of the double who had been in the scene with Jerry. They rehearsed the scene one more time, and the director seemed satisfied.

Everything seemed to take so long. Lights had to be adjusted and moved, cameras set; the makeup man touched up Melissa's face and wiped off a spot of perspiration. The hairdresser swept in and smoothed out her set, and then they were ready.

42

"Quiet on the set. This is a take," the assistant director said.

"Roll sound," the director said.

"Sound rolling and speed."

"Slate it."

"And . . . action!"

Mark stood perfectly still during the shot. It was less than fifteen seconds before the director yelled "cut," and he swore for another twenty seconds before he told Jerry what the trouble was this time.

Mark moved cautiously toward the big door he had come in, but now it was closed. A guard on a small door nearby waved him forward.

"If you want out, now's the time before the red light comes on again."

Mark slipped through the door and walked quickly back to his car in the visitors' lot. He wished he could saunter around the whole back lot with his badge on and see lots of things, but there was no time now. Maybe later. Perhaps he could come back with Joey and have lunch in the commissary and see some stars.

Mark drove back into Los Angeles on the San Diego Freeway and got off at Westwood and the UCLA campus. He found the track and watched it for a few minutes but saw nothing of the famous actor. Mark changed clothes in the car, putting on a pair of khaki shorts, a T-shirt, and some Nike Waffle Trainer running shoes. He locked everything else in the car and put his ignition key in the small pocket of his shorts.

Mark had done four easy laps around the quarter-mile track before he saw the man come onto the oval. His T-shirt was already soaked through, water dripped off the back of his hair, and he was puffing. Mark slowed, and when he was sure the man was Brad Russell, he fell into step beside him.

"Hey, runner, how's it going?" Mark asked.

"Just getting in my six. I'm not the real runner; that's Bruce Dern. This damn thing seems to get longer every day. How far you going?"

"Four if I'm lucky. I'm out of shape."

They jogged a quarter of a mile around the track, and Mark could tell Brad was getting winded.

"Want to walk a lap?"

"Hell, no! I might slow down, but I never walk."

A hundred yards on Mark tried again. "Look, you wouldn't be mad if I told you I came down here hunting you, would you?"

"Hell, no. When I don't get recognized, that's when I get mad."

"Good. I'm not a reporter or a fan magazine snoop. I don't want to write anything or tell anyone anything. What I'm trying to do is pound a couple of nails in a coffin, and you can help me."

Brad laughed. "Sounds like fun. Anyone I know?"

"Yes. It's an outfit called GTA."

"Oh." Brad scowled. "And you're wondering about the wreck."

"No, I think I know what happened. The truth is you couldn't have lived through that crash. Which means somebody put you in the car after it hit and before the cops got there."

Brad looked over at him. "Hey, you a cop?"

"No, not even a private eye. I'm working on my own. Do you know what happened out there that night?"

"Not exactly, but somebody slugged me from behind when I got out of the car. I came to in the backseat of my Rolls. I was tied up. When the car stopped, they got me out, stood me up, and made me watch as they rolled the car over the cliff with Jan still inside it. The

44

sons of bitches killed her and wanted me to know I was next. They slugged me again, and the next thing I knew I woke up inside the wreck, and somebody was working down the cliff toward me."

"Could you identify any of them?"

"No way. It was dark and they had masks. I saw at least three of them, but no way I could ID them."

"They knew there would be a murder charge hanging over them. But they let you watch. Meaning they were pros who knew what they were doing."

"One of them was blond, I think."

"That could help. I'd really like to nail these rats."

"I'll help any way I can, but keep my name out of it. The police still have a sneaky hunch I planned the whole thing to kill Jan. No way. She was the best thing to happen to me for a long time."

"I won't involve you, Brad."

"Good. I don't want any more trouble with those goons. They all looked like exfootball players."

"I know the type. You think of anything else you can tell me? Did you see another car? Hear any voices? Did they slip and use a name?"

They jogged another half-lap, and Brad shook his head. "No way I come up with anything more to help. The guy down at GTA who signed me was a cool one, but he wouldn't have been in on any of the strong-arm stuff. He isn't the type."

"Johnathan Westerly?"

Brad looked over quickly. "Yeah. You met him?"

"This morning. Brad, anything you can think of that might help, I'll appreciate. I'm digging up the whole county if I have to. I want to hang that bunch out to dry for twenty years."

"I'll go along with that. They let Jan die without one damn word. Without a thought, just to pressure me."

45

He looked at Mark, slowed down, and they walked. "Damn, you aren't even sweating yet or breathing hard."

"I will; I warm up slow," Mark said.

"Yeah, sure you do, after twenty miles. I bet your heartbeat right now is about sixty. Mine is 150. There aren't a lot of guys out here in as good a shape as you're in." He looked around the edges of the track. "Be sure and watch your ass out here. Sometimes they send some jerk in a suit to watch me work out. I don't think he's here today, but just don't walk around any corners quickly. Know what I mean?"

"Thanks, Brad, I'll watch it. If you think of anything else that might help, call 452-9111. It's a drop where you can leave a message for me."

Brad Russell wiped sweat from his forehead and said he'd call. "Damn, I've got three more laps to do; I better get with it. Good luck." He took off at a slow jog, talking to himself, psyching himself up for another three-quarters of a mile.

Mark ran back to his car, saw no one around it, and changed back into his long pants.

Beverly Hills is near the Westwood campus. Mark found Ladyflower Lane and the 2323 address. It was a big place with a painted adobe wall across the front closed in by an iron gate at one side. He could see little of the place, but it appeared to be a Spanish hacienda with a courtyard. Mark parked along the street half a block from the house and waited. Within fifteen minutes he saw two different catering trucks arrive and go through the gate. A short time later a sound system truck arrived.

It was just after three o'clock. Mark drove to a filling station down on Santa Monica Boulevard and called Joey.

"You know anything about a bash going down at Lorna Luna's place tonight? I just saw some catering trucks and a sound van go in there."

"Oh, yeah, right. I saw it in the trades a couple of days ago. She's throwing a small party for her director on *The Long Night*. It's some kind of a PR thing, probably. There should be lots of people there, but I don't know how I can get you an invitation. Hers always have a little magnetic-coded card that you put in a slot in her front door after you get through the main gate."

"No problem; I'll bluff my way in. Remember when it starts?"

"Anywhere from cocktails at six-thirty I'd say."

"Black tie?"

"In Hollywood? You've got to be joking. A mink sweatshirt would be over dressing for a Lorna Luna party."

"Thanks, I'll drop by."

That night at seven o'clock Mark parked two blocks from Lorna's house. That was as close as he could get. The Beverly Hills street was jammed with flashy cars. He walked to the main gate and began rummaging through his pockets. The guard standing near the open iron barricade did not smile.

"Don't tell me—you've lost your invitation."

"Can't seem to find it." Mark wore flared slacks and a sleek Hawaiian flowered shirt.

"Better move along then; nobody crashes a Luna party. The Beverly Hills cops will be past here in three minutes. They take good care of Lorna. So far they've run in three loiterers on this block. She's got the chief in her back pocket."

"I could drop a twenty-dollar bill," Mark said.

"I would get fired if I picked it up."

Mark nodded. Maybe he'd found an honest man. He walked down to the end of the wall, back the way he'd come, and when the guard looked the other way, Mark jumped into the unwalled yard next door. He waited a minute behind some shrubs and a tall twisted juniper.

Three minutes later Mark had climbed the wall along the side of the Luna property, jumped down in the shrubs and plants there, and gradually worked around to the patio at the back of the house where a barbecue was in progress. He filtered into the back lawn, picked a drink off a champagne tray, and mingled.

There were thirty people on the lighted patio giving the cook unwanted advice. They were mostly well-dressed, and Mark recognized some movie and TV faces without being able to put names to them. He did pick out Carol and Sally and thought he saw Gary Cooper until he remembered that Cooper had been dead since 1961.

Mark moved through the wide glass doors into a huge living room that was packed with people. It wasn't a courtyard-hacienda-type house at all. The living room was decorated in white and black with a zebra motif. In one corner near a heatless fireplace, he found the hostess, surrounded by a dozen people. Mark edged into the group and heard the woman in the striking red dress called Lorna. He knew he was at the right spot. Her voice dominated the gathering.

"But, darling, I'm simply too old for you," Lorna said to a young man beside her. "I know it and you know it and the movie-going public knows it. No, I'm simply going to have to admit that I'm past thirty now or find a leading man who is right for me, young enough to attract the audiences but who seems to be emotionally mature enough to be able to cope with the realities of an old bitch like me."

Everyone laughed, including Lorna. Someone moved, and Mark found himself in the front row, only six feet from the famous Lorna Luna. She was about forty-five, but two face-lifts had eliminated the wrinkles. Her makeup was professionally sleek, her brown hair freshly set, and her body as shapely as any of the slinky starlets who were jiggling around, casually breast-bumping into every important director or producer they could spot. Lorna caught Mark's eye and smiled.

"Jesus H. Kreist, look at him. It's a manna from heaven. Thank you, God. Look at that face. Now there is the kind of man I was talking about. He could be my next leading man. Look at him!" Lorna walked up to Mark and kissed his lips, stepped back, and smiled. "Oh, lord, yes! He's got the qualities I couldn't describe. Darling, I'm no good with words unless someone writes me a marvelous script. But you've got the dark handsomeness, the touch of a real bastard, the black eyes of the devil, a face that's rugged and appealing and will wow them even in Butte, Montana. What's your name, darling?"

Mark tried to keep a smile from his face. Instead he let a touch of a frown tinge his features.

"Lance Lansing, Miss Luna."

"Isn't that sweet? Lance. I like it, and it has Freudian symbolism that we all can think about." Everyone laughed. She put her arm through his. "Now, let me give you the guided tour, Lance. I just finished redecorating the whole place, and I insist on showing you everything, including the queen's bedroom. I refuse to call it a master bedroom, and the madam's bedroom sounds too suggestive."

49

They went into a dining room that was forty feet long and cleared for disco dancing. A five-piece combo beat out a disco rhythm in the far corner.

"I don't remember you on the invitation list, Lance. Did you come with someone?"

"No, I jumped the fence and came through the patio."

She laughed and nodded. "Yes, you just might have at that. You have more intensity than any actor I've seen. Are you an actor or what?"

"I wanted to talk to you, and this seemed the quickest way. I understand you're represented by GTA."

He felt her hand on his arm tighten for a moment, then relax. Her face hadn't changed. She was a marvelous actress if she were trying to hide something.

"Yes, GTA has me. I was with the first small agency they bought almost a year ago. They've treated me fairly."

"How else could they? You're sure you're not having any kind of trouble with them at all?"

"Trouble? Oh, not really." She sighed. "Well, maybe a little."

"How little?"

"They want me to renegotiate my contract with them and to give them personal management and PR representation as well. That would be another ten percent for them."

"But you'd rather not do that?"

"I've had loyal friends doing those jobs for me for fifteen years. I can't just shut them out now."

"But GTA is pressing. Have they gotten physical with you at all, threatened you?"

"Oh, goodness, no." She paused. "Why do you ask?"

"I know some stars who haven't been that lucky." Mark took out a card the professor had printed for him. "I'm Lance Lansing, special investigator for the Senate special antitrust subcommittee. We're interested in the sudden grabbing up of most of the major stars in Hollywood by one machine. It's my job to see if there's a cause for antitrust or even criminal action."

"Oh, hell. I hoped you were an actor, a good one I could get into my next film. It would have been great. So you are a real investigator. I'm just positive that I can't help you. Somebody down at the office talked to me one day and said they were interested in getting the PR and management. I told them I was happy with things the way they were, and they dropped it. I don't think they plan to bring it up again. And they weren't unpleasant about it. My goodness, no."

"'At least you aren't afraid to talk about them. Would you help me if you can, Miss Luna? Would you give me a phone call if they even hint at violence, or if you hear of them using violence on anyone else in town?"

"Oh, I don't know. Yes, I guess I should do that. I'm not going to get involved in anything illegal, or so that I would have to testify. Of course I'll cooperate with you. The fact is there's one of their top executives here tonight. He's a vice president or something. I don't even remember his name. I'll point him out to you."

They walked into another room, where she looked around and led him to the table loaded with hot and cold hors d'oeuvres. He was positioned at the tray of tiny blintzes.

"He's the man with no hair and a blue tie," she said.

"Maybe I should talk with him," Mark said. "Miss

51

Luna, thank you for your help, and if you ever need any aid from me, or have anything to tell me, call me."

Mark moved away, took a small pad from his pocket, and wrote a quick note. It said: "Trouble. Get down to the office as soon as you can." There was no signature.

Mark had one of the waiters give the note to the man with the blue tie. He watched and saw the bald head nod once. The man took another sweet-and-sour meatball and headed for the front door. Mark was just behind him. Once outside the gate Mark sprinted for his car and drove up just as the other man rolled out of the parking area in front of the house in a Lincoln Continental.

It was a simple tail job. The man never checked behind him once. Less than five minutes later the GTA man stopped in a no-parking area in front of a small building among the Century City skyscrapers. He went in a side door, and Mark watched lights flash on in the second floor center. Mark noted the position of the lights and decided that he would come back and investigate the building later when there was no one there to see him. He caught the firm name on the big front windows: Investments Unlimited.

Chapter 5

HICKS NIX SLICK TRICKS PIX

At seven o'clock the next morning Mark called Joey Larson at the motel number. The hostelry switchboard girl said there was no one by that name registered.

"Joey Larson. He was there for two days," Mark said. "If he's not there, when did he check out?"

"Just a min, honey, I'll check. Righto, now I see it. He cut out last night about five o'clock. Paid his bill and left."

"Thanks," Mark said and hung up. He remembered the number he had used for Joey's business office and dialed it. Joey must have gotten tired waiting around and gone back to check his mail. The phone in Joey's office rang six times, seven, eight. Mark hung on, Joey had to be there. At last someone picked up the receiver.

"Yes, hello," a woman's voice said.

Mark frowned. "Is this the Joey Larson Talent Agency?"

"Oh, yes, that's right."

"Who are you?"

"Oh, I'm Joey's secretary."

"Joey doesn't have a secretary. He can't afford one. Is Joey there? I need to talk to him right away."

Mark heard a sniffle. "Young lady, who are you? Is anything wrong?"

"Yes, something is dreadfully wrong. Are you Joey's friend?"

"Yes, an old, long-time friend."

"Then I wish you'd come right over. You know where his office is?"

Mark said he'd never been there. She gave him the address and told him how to find it. Mark left at once.

It was one of those little offices that must once have been a private home out on the far end of Sunset Boulevard. The paint was not new, and the front door opened directly from the sidewalk and had been cut in half to form a Dutch door so the top could be left open and the bottom half closed. Mark knocked on the 8080 number plate, and the door opened inward at once.

She was young, attractive, and Mexican.

"Hello, I'm Angelina Perez. I've been working on a case with Joey, and he told me to meet him here this morning. When I came, the door was closed but unlocked. When Joey didn't answer, I came on in. Joey liked pizza for breakfast, and I guessed he went out for some and would be right back."

She seemed to run the words and sentences together. Mark had a feeling she kept talking so she wouldn't break down and cry again. He saw a tear stain on her soft brown cheeks, and another tear seeped out.

She was about five-six, maybe a 115 pounds, with a slender figure, and dark hair cut short. Her brown eyes looked straight up at Mark. She had changed and now had a stern, professional mask on.

"Somebody killed Joey. Two shots from behind, close range."

54

Mark took it like a kick in the stomach. He scowled and looked around the small office. He hadn't expected this. He guessed Joey had been beaten up, hurt, but was not dead.

"Where is he?"

"Over here."

Mark found Joey sitting on the floor in the corner behind his desk. His hands were folded in his lap. His head sagged forward. Powder burns slightly singed the hair around the two small holes in the back of his head.

"Silencer, held close," Mark said. "The silencer eliminated most of the powder burns, but there are still a few."

"They moved him over here so he'd be less obvious to anyone looking inside," Angelina said.

Mark glanced up, watching the pretty Chicano. "You sound like a cop. Are you?"

"I'm a licensed private investigator. I was working with Joey on a case. I guess that's all academic."

"To Joey it is, but it might not be to your client."

"Should we call the police?"

"Yes, but first, do you know if anything is stolen? Is Joey's wallet in his pocket? Any files ransacked? Was it a robbery or just a complicated little murder?"

"I haven't touched anything. I've never been involved with a murder case before. Dead people usually frighten me, but Joey doesn't. I find it hard to believe that Joey's . . ."

"Are you sure you didn't touch anything?"

"Oh, the doorknob."

"And the telephone," Mark said. He made a quick inspection of the small office. He wiped off the phone and did the same to the doorknob inside, not cleaning

55

it entirely, but ruining any of Angie's prints that might have been there. The killer would have worn gloves. There was no mess in the room, nothing obviously missing. He looked at the girl. She wore a sleek brown pants suit and a brown scarf around her throat. A white blouse was buttoned high. Her purse was a matching brown and big enough to hold a gun. She was beautiful.

"Angelina, we can't do the police any good here, so we're leaving. Do you have a hat?" She shook her head. "Is there a back door out of here?"

"No. Joey said he should have one, but there isn't any."

"Then we'll both go out the front door and walk away as inconspicuously as possible. We don't want anyone to tie us in with Joey's doorway this morning. I'll swing the door inward and wipe off our prints; then we leave quickly and walk to the left towards my car. I hope you're not parked right in front?"

She said she wasn't.

"Good. We get out, go in my car somewhere for breakfast or coffee, and then we'll talk. I have a lot of questions."

"Thank you. You'd think after all the training I had I wouldn't just freeze up. I've seen DBs before."

"It wasn't that, Angelina. Joey was your friend, and that makes all the difference. Now let's get out of here."

No one seemed to pay any attention to them as they left the front door and walked to Mark's car. They got in and he drove away, stopping at the first phone booth he spotted to call the LAPD.

"Sergeant? I just heard some shots coming from 8080 Sunset. Some guy ran out, but I didn't get a good look at him. I think somebody got killed. Yeah, at 8080 Sunset. I'm going back and take a look!" Mark hung up quickly before the cop could ask him his name.

Ten minutes later Mark found a restaurant, and they went in. As the strain faded from her face, Mark found her more and more attractive. Her brown eyes were turning from shock to anger.

"What were you doing for Joey?" Mark asked.

"I can't tell you . . . oh, I have no more client relationship. It doesn't matter. He was my client. I was doing a work-up for him on an organization called Global Talent Agency. They were pushing Joey around, pressuring him to sell a contract on his biggest actor."

"Yes, on Randy Smith." He watched her surprise show through. Mark wondered if she were a plant, a clever actress GTA hired to "find" the body and see who came and what happened. She could intercept any trouble. She could be a spy, but he doubted it. He'd watched too many people lie. He knew the signs, the methods, the effects it had on people that they never felt. If she were lying, she was the best little actress in town.

"Angelina, could I see your PI card and your weapons permit?"

"Sure." She took a billfold from her purse and handed him three cards. One was her private investigator's license from the state. Another her police identification card every PI needed. And the third was her Los Angeles County Sheriff's office license to carry a concealed weapon. She also showed him a duplicated copy of her discharge from the LAPD and a copy of her CIA identification card.

"CIA?" Mark asked.

"For two years after my training. Field agent. Then my mother got sick, and I had to come home to take care of her, so I got a special hardship discharge. It worked out for the best that way. Mom's gone now, but it helped her because I was here. Then I opened my own agency, and after a year it's starting to meet expenses."

She sipped coffee from a heavy mug and stared at him across the wisps of steam. "Now you know all about me, but I don't even know who you are."

He handed her his Senate Investigating Committee card. She read it and smiled.

"You use a good quality printer, I can say that. I hadn't thought of the investigating committee dodge. That's a good one. I meet lots of people, and I always make it a point to save their cards. So far I've collected about two hundred. Give me five minutes in my file, and I can come up with a card for almost anything."

She handed him a card from her purse, and she was Helen Borthwick, interior designer from Beverly Hills.

"You don't buy the idea that I work for the Senate Subcommittee?" Mark asked.

"Not for a second. You're not the organization man type. They taught us how to size up a person in training, remember? For you I'd put down: Six-feet-two inches. Two-hundred-and-five pounds. Dark complexioned, perhaps mixed blood of Indian or Mexican with gringo. Moves like a jungle cat, excellent balance, lithe, agile. Heavily muscled. Eyes black, bottomless. Wears a black moustache that's real. Black hair a little longer than most of the men wear now that ears are starting to make a comeback. Age, about twenty-eight. Something of a loner, likes to work by himself. The sports jacket is well-cut to conceal the shoulder leather, but I

58

can see the outline of a piece there, probably not a .38 police special. My guess is some kind of a lightweight .45. Now, could I see your PI card and your permit to pack?"

Mark felt his growing agitation with this pretty lady giving way to admiration. She was sharp, smart, and street wise.

"Lady, you must have been one hell of a good cop."

"I was. That's why I was invited to join the CIA. Anyway they needed another double minority, female and Mexican. I was a good agent, too." She grinned. "You don't have a license for that cannon, do you?"

"Nope, never got around to it."

"Besides, you couldn't get one if you tried, and you don't like the vibes inside any police building, right?"

"I don't know where you get your tea leaves . . ."

"But they read about right, don't they?"

"Too damn close."

"Look, when I talked to Joey, he was in the office. That was late last night. He said somebody tried to nail him when he arrived. So he had to stay inside until the people went away, or he had to call in the cops. He wasn't worried at all about getting blown away. He said he had protection. He told me an old college buddy from UCLA by the name of Mark was helping him on the GTA thing. So I can only guess that you're Mark. I don't know what's in it for you, but I'm staying on the case. Sure, my client is dead, and so is my paycheck, but I'm on the case until I find out who killed Joey. I owe him that much. So why don't we pool our information? Two heads better and all. Who knows? Maybe we can work together on this one."

"You were right, Angelina . . ."

"Hey, Mark. My friends cut that down to Angie."

"Good, Angie. You were right. I'm not an organization man. I work alone. And right now, instead of a vague strong-arm racket, I've got a murder one that's just wiped out an old friend."

"I'll even buy you breakfast," Angie said. "What can it hurt? I'll stay out of your way if you're worried about that. And I can take care of myself. I've dug up a little bit on the case, and I do know a lot of people in Hollywood. Contacts, phone numbers. I specialize in the show biz end of this town."

Mark reached over and picked up her brown purse. It was heavy.

"Do you mind?" Without waiting for her to answer he unsnapped the clasp and looked inside. In the first compartment Mark found what he was hunting and laughed softly.

"Well, I'll be damned, a Detonics .45. That's one gold star in your favor. But I still work alone. I might ask you some questions from time to time. Do you have a phone number?"

"Sure, do you? I'll trade."

He stared at her eyes, which were now laughing at him. But he saw much more: a beautiful girl who could take care of herself or she never would have made it through field-agent training with the CIA. A girl who could help him on this case now that his inside contact man was dead.

"Okay, Angie, it's a trade. No promises, but a contact." He gave her his phone number. "Don't try to trace back and find out an address to go with that. It's a blind drop I can trust, and it's the end of the road in a search."

"Your drop is fine with me. Mine is an answering service."

It was her turn to smile.

Their breakfast came, and she grabbed the check.

"No promises," Mark said.

Her level gaze met his squarely. "No promises."

Chapter 6

DAY FOR NIGHT: DOUBLE PRINT

Jeffrey Scott Duncann sat in the den of his Beverly Hills mansion. He clamped his teeth down hard on a five-dollar cigar and swore under his breath. Then he talked again into the French-style telephone.

"Dammit, Marcel, you know me. Have I ever treated you badly? Come on, Marcel. I gave you work when you needed it. I kept you off unemployment for five years. Now all I want is for you to put together one goddamned crew for me."

Marcel Linker, one of the best production managers in Hollywood, was stalling. They both knew it.

"Look, J.S., I appreciate what you've done for me. But now I'm the one asked to do a favor. Let me do it my way. We simply set the whole thing up as an independent production. Your name never has to be mentioned."

"No! Christ, Marcel. What are you doing to me? What do you think I am, a leper or something? I've been in this business for thirty years. My name must mean something out there."

"J.S., you know exactly what it means right now. You're poison. Let's face it, J.S. If I went out to hire a crew for a picture under your production banner, I couldn't get shit. Now you know that, J.S. You've been trying to cast for six months on the sequel to *Starbound*. Why don't you just relax and let things cool off for another six months or a year? Take a cruise around the world, get married and fight, anything. Then later we do the sequel as an independent production, and gradually you can work back into the business. You gave the whole industry a black eye, J.S. You've got to give the people time to forget and forgive."

"I want back in business right now, Marcel!"

"It won't work right now, J.S."

"Marcel, I'm a producer. I've made the biggest hit of the decade with *Starbound Space War*. People should be knocking down my door trying to get on board for the next two or three sequels."

"J.S., this is like a bad movie script. You know damn well why you're on the blacklist. Hell, you don't need the money. Buy a motor home, and drive around Europe and Italy. Have some fun. Relax and enjoy yourself."

"I enjoy myself only when I'm working myself to death. You know how that is, Marcel."

"So work to death on an independent. Back me with two million, and I'll turn you out a money-making Good Old Boys Car-Chase picture for the summer drive-ins."

"No. I have to be the head man. I won't work for anyone else."

"Then work with me? Just behind the scenes."

"No."

"I'm sorry, J.S. You do it this way, or I'd guess it will take you five years to get back into the business. But it's your life. Call me anytime. I've got to go. Goodbye, J.S."

Jeffrey Scott Duncann, J.S. to millions of his fans

and workers in the film industry, put down the phone. For a fraction of a second he wanted to cry, but he shook himself out of the role he had been playing. He heaved up from the softly upholstered chair, roaring with glee at his clever deception. He had been properly sniveling. He had crawled just enough, yet maintained his position. By morning the story would be all over Hollywood, that the great J.S. Duncann had struck out again, that he had begged Marcel Linker to get up a crew for him for the sequel to the biggest grossing picture of the year, and Linker had said no.

Linker was not the kind of man to let such an ego booster go unnoticed. He was perfect for the part; he'd spread the word fast.

J.S. chomped on the cigar. Damn right he had done a good job with Linker. Now nobody would wonder what he was doing all this time that he couldn't produce. Sure he could go to Italy, but that was running away. He wanted to produce here. Now nobody would try to connect him with any other action underway in Hollywood.

Duncann still hated them. He hated all the two-faced, fair-weather friends who had been so quick to condemn him. Hell, they had done worse themselves; they just never had been caught.

He thought back. Things hadn't been that bad. True, he was a little short on cash flow when the *Starbound Space War* film had cost so much. It had gone over twenty million and drained off most of his liquid funds.

Sure he had written a few floater checks. So what if he had signed a name or two that weren't his? Nobody got hurt. The only problem came when the damned W-2 statement of wages form went out listing that damn seventy-five thousand dollars in fees paid to Dirk Stone. Stone was not much at the box office now, but he had been very big five years ago. He hadn't done any work for Duncann Productions for two years, so he questioned the W-2 form, and some damn clerk at Duncann Productions had shown him the signed and returned check.

Then Stone knew something was wrong, and he actually came and confronted J.S. about it. Hell, what could he say? Just a little mix-up, a minor shortage in one of the funds that had to be taken care of quickly. He knew Stone wouldn't mind. But the press got hold of it and then the district attorney. Restitution was made, and Stone didn't press charges. But the newspapers kept punching at it, playing on the forgery issue, and before it died down, three other actors had come up with similar irregularities in their pay records.

Jeffrey Scott Duncann finally held a press conference and bared his soul to the world. Yes, he said, he might have broken a few rules but nothing serious. He paid all four men the amount of the original checks drawn to them. Nobody pressed the forgery charges, and the problem seemed to be a dead issue.

Duncann didn't count on it being an election year. The Los Angeles district attorney was up for reelection against a tough opponent, and he launched a full-scale investigation of the case. Witnesses were called, and the whole thing had another blast of bad press.

The end result was three weeks of daily bad publicity for J.S. and his Duncann Productions. There were no indictments, and no formal charges brought. But Hollywood is a strange, small community of top filmmakers. It's an intimate group of talented producers, directors, writers, and stars. Suddenly Duncann Productions was the outlaw of the group. Within a week, two Duncann Productions were shut down because top directors quit or were fired and could not be replaced.

It wasn't a formal boycott, nor was it a blacklist as was used against certain communist-tinged writers in Hollywood in the '50s. But the word was out that Duncann Productions was off limits. Within a month nobody who was anybody would work for Duncann unless they were finishing an ironbound contract that couldn't be broken.

Final editing was then underway on *Starbound Space War,* and the editors knew they had a winner. They wouldn't quit for any reason. By the time the movie was ready for distribution, it had such good advance notices that every movie house available was used for the grand premiere, and it was a roaring, smashing, instant success.

Money was not a factor. Duncann had been a tremendously rich man for years with much real estate, business properties, diversified businesses and stocks and bonds. But now with the new millions rolling in from *Starbound,* he had the urge to fight back at Hollywood's boycott and its blackmail.

But still no one would work for him. A call for dancers in *Variety* would bring in two hundred as long as it was a blind ad. But the same ad run a week later with a Duncann Productions logo would turn up fifteen or twenty beginning hoofers.

Slowly the idea came to him. He knew how he could make Hollywood pay, make every producer in the country who had blacklisted him get down on his knees and beg for mercy. Oh, it would be sweet!

Duncann set up a new corporation with hidden ownership and bought one talent agency. He quickly moved in on three more, and before Hollywood knew it, his company had six of the biggest stars under contract. He called the firm the Global Talent Agency, and it had no connection with Duncann Productions or any of his subsidiaries. After that it was easy. Now he was picking up the last of the holdouts. Ten or fifteen more and he would have the two hundred biggest names in show business under his representation.

Then just let anyone try to produce. Just let them have a go at it. He would make such fantastic salary demands that the producers would be unable to pay.

J.S. Duncann leaned back in his chair and puffed on the long cigar. That was going to be a great day. He would throw a party and invite everyone who was anyone in Hollywood to come, all in the name of GTA so they would show up. Then he would announce the basic salary scales for his actors and actresses, and while the producers and directors were still surprised and wounded, he would walk to center stage with a travel spot on him all the way. He would tell them that he owned GTA, and not a one of them would get any talent from his agency. He'd see the producers all starve or move to Italy first. All they had to do was get back in his favor, and they could do that by crawling back and asking his forgiveness for the ugly way they had treated him this past year.

Oh, yes, that would be a great day! He decided it might happen within a month, six weeks at least. Until then all he had to do was sit back and wait.

For a moment he thought of the wild story that Westerly told him on the phone from the GTA headquarters. Something about an actor who came in for an interview but who turned out to be an expert at judo or something and beat up both Westerly's bodyguards and knocked him out. The man left a chipped blue flint arrowhead on his desk. Westerly was frightened to death and demanded better protection.

J.S. had laughed at him. Westerly was an idiot and a closet queen. It wasn't fashionable any more to brag that you were gay. Hundreds of the fags in Hollywood had quietly stolen back into their closets. J.S. snorted. That was where they belonged.

Duncann walked to the window. Hilda, his German masseuse, was waiting at the poolside. It was time for his swim and a good rubdown. He smiled. Hilda knew all the right places to rub. He waddled toward the door, his Hitchcock-type figure already anticipating the talented fingers of the German girl. He spoke no German and she no English. He liked it best that way.

On the way to the pool he pulled off his clothes and let them fall. One of the maids would pick them up. At the pool edge he dove into the water with a large splash. As he broke the surface, he saw Hilda at the far end. She had slid out of her bikini and dove in as well.

Momentarily he thought about the tall, dark man Westerly had described. Was there any way he could be a threat? J.S. snorted at the thought. No one could threaten him now.

He turned over on his back as he felt Hilda near. She glided up beside him in the water. Yes, it was going to be a good day.

Chapter 7

STUNTMAN'S KILL SHOT

The day Joey was shot to death turned out to be the most unproductive one Mark had experienced so far in Hollywood. Meeting Angie Perez had been the only bright spot. He left her early that morning and tried to contact three more movie stars who were under contract with GTA, but he was rebuffed on each attempt.

Mark waited impatiently until dark, hoping his luck would change. He had no new leads, no theories to check out. He was dry. The cover of darkness should provide him with a chance to find some ammunition to use against GTA. At least he hoped that he could find something useful.

By six-thirty an early evening onshore drift had brought a marine layer of clouds off the Pacific Ocean and flooded the Los Angeles area with a massive wet fog blanket. Everything was gray and damp.

Mark parked two blocks from the Sunset Boulevard headquarters of GTA and slid into the alley directly behind the building. The thick fog meant he could see only twenty feet away. He scanned the back of the building, a two-floor affair, looking for an open window. He tried the door, spotted the dead bolt, and knew he couldn't open it.

On his second check of windows, he saw that the third one over the second floor was open a crack. It had to be unlocked. Mark climbed up the vertical side of the stucco and frame building. It was harder than climbing a brick building, but he found small hand-holds and cracks for his toes and worked up the wall to the second floor like a spider. He reached the window and tested it. Unlocked. The Penetrator pushed the glass upward, rolled across the window sill, and lit on his hands and knees inside the office.

It was dark. He remained still on the carpeted floor listening. Nothing. Mark came to his feet, his night vision showing him all he needed to know about the room. It was an office devoted to Debbie Dean and her fantastic dancing routines. Full-sized pictures of the star in a dozen costumes papered the walls. Mark moved silently to the door and opened it. The hallway was carpeted, dimly lighted. The Penetrator began an intensive, silent search of each room and office.

After an hour he had found nothing. The Penetrator worked with his *Sho-tu-ça* night sight, an ancient Cheyenne dog-soldier method of combining psychology, mind over matter, and religion to give him night sight as good as a normal eye has at early dusk. Only rarely did he need to use his penlight to check the writing on some papers.

In one office he found a complete listing of the stars and actors now under contract to GTA. There were over three hundred individuals. Most he had never heard of, but the list was sprinkled with top-quality people and stars he knew. GTA had a stranglehold on the industry. All they had to do was cut off everyone at once or play one producer against the others.

On the first floor Mark came to a familiar room. It was where he had met Johnathan Westerly. The room had no outside windows. Mark used his pen flash freely here. He picked the lock on one filing cabinet and went through the contents slowly. There had to be something here he could use.

The list at first looked like any other employee group, but it was set up by services: secretarial, reception, guards, PR specialists, interviewers, a dozen other categories. At the ed of the list were two names under "Special Assistants to the Manager." Johnathan Westerly was the manager. Mark looked at the names again and memorized the names of the two special assistants. They were Keith Zilke and Wade Kennedy. He had a hunch they could be the muscle men.

The Penetrator went to the big executive desk and began a systematic check of each drawer. When he was sure there was nothing in a drawer that would help him, Mark dumped the contents on the floor.

In the third drawer he found a possible. It was a folder marked "Contacts." Inside were four telephone numbers. Mark memorized them, reading them over three times each, permanently engraving them on his memory circuits so they could be recalled on command. He had just trashed another drawer and turned to drop it on the floor when he saw a .38 muzzle aimed at him from the open office doorway. The guard was in his fifties, probably an excop, Mark decided in an instant. He would know how to use the weapon but would use due caution. Under the uniform garrison cap, the man's face frowned.

"What the hell? Get your hands up, young man, and don't move anything else. Thought I heard something up here."

Mark did as he was told. There would be a chance to disarm him later. Mark didn't want a shot fired. He

71

had no argument with the guard, who probably was an innocent sheep among the wolves.

"Okay, friend. Come out from there slow like. I want a good look at you." The room was still in semi-darkness. He reached for the switch for the overhead light beside the door. Mark saw the movement and knew the cop would be blinded for a moment. When the light came on, Mark threw the empty desk drawer at the gunhand. The wooden drawer slammed against the man's arm, jolting the weapon out of his hand. Mark ran for the gun and got it before the guard could. The Penetrator motioned the man to the couch in the big office.

Mark didn't speak as he taped the man's ankles together with black, stretchy electricians' tape. Then he taped the man's wrists together behind his back and let the guard lie down on the couch.

Still without a word, Mark went back and finished searching and trashing the office but found nothing else he thought he could use. At least he had the four phone numbers and the names of two men who might be the outfit's muscle. It was a good two hour's work.

Mark told the guard to rest easy; his replacement would find him on the next shift. Mark took the rounds out of the .38 and left it on the desk. The Penetrator didn't worry about fingerprints this time; he had on his semipermeable, skintight, plastic gloves that left a perfect set of invented fingerprints that had been carefully crafted into the plastic.

He left by a first-floor window, closing it after he was out and dropping to the ground. Mark jogged back to his car and drove away. The fog was still as thick as when he came.

Mark didn't worry about the guard identifying him. The man had seen his face only briefly when he snapped on the light, and Mark had been moving. He'd turned off the overhead before he tied up the guard, so there was no problem there.

His next stop on his dark hours tour of Hollywood was a building in Century City, then home of Investments Unlimited. There would be more secuirty there, Mark was sure. He just didn't know what and whether they would be sheep or goats.

The Penetrator parked a block away and studied the building for a few minutes as the fog began to lift. There was a rent-a-cop in the small lobby and a sign-in sheet. Mark might bluff his way through and sign in, but the guard would take a good look at him and remember his face. No, there had to be a better way.

Mark tried the back and side doors. All were locked with some type of electric bolt system that he couldn't pick. He walked around the back of the structure again and saw no other entrances. There was only an electric panel and a telephone access door. Access door?

Mark walked past it slowly and saw that it was an entry for telephone servicing. He stopped and tried the handle. It had a simple tumbler lock. The Penetrator knelt and in twenty seconds had the lock open. He pulled the door back and stepped inside. A small passageway led upward, probably to the roof. Mark took the metal steps three at a time, his night vision still functioning. At the top of the stairs he found a door with a lock on the inside. He opened it, left it unlocked, and stepped to the roof.

A quick survey showed him another access door. It was in the center of the building and must go down. The Penetrator picked the simple lock and cautiously eased open the door. Down a half flight of steps he came to a large storeroom. It would be offices someday when it was rented and finished. Right now it was the empty third floor of the building.

The Penetrator went through an unlocked door into a hallway and down steps to the second floor. Here the area was carpeted, painted, slickly furnished. Investments Unlimited had the whole second floor.

The Penetrator found a reception area just opposite the elevator. On the other side of that section were the executive offices. None was locked. The largest, best-furnished office turned out to be that of the president. So far Mark hadn't seen a single guard or night watch-man.

Hardin knew what he was looking for this time. The man from GTA at the party had reacted to Mark's note to come to the "office" right away. He had gone to Investments Unlimited. Why? Mark searched the locked files, hunting company books, legal records, anything that might show the purpose, the actual business, or the ownership of Investments Unlimited.

He found nothing of value in the locked files. Evidently there was a certain amount of investment business carried on, but there didn't seem to be many clients.

Mark sat down at the president's desk once more and opened the drawers. In the top one, in a basket marked "Today," the Penetrator found what he wanted: the Investments Unlimited annual report to stockholders.

On the second page was a complete listing of costs, income, and deficits built up so far by GTA. The agency was a wholly owned subsidiary of Investments Unlimited. That made sense. Now Mark felt he was getting somewhere. All he had to do was find out who owned the investing firm.

They should have nailed him easily. If they had used

the guns in their belts, they would have. But the pair were smashers and crushers, brute force amateurs, not seasoned hit men. They both burst into the office together, planted their feet, and guarded the only door. One flipped a switch that turned on indirect lights.

"Who the hell are you?" the taller, blond one asked.

Mark recognized him at once, the goon who had frightened Joey in the bar. Mark wondered if he were the one who had killed Joey and broken Melissa Martindale's arm.

The Penetrator didn't answer as the second, slightly smaller man began to shift to the left to put Mark between them. Hardin knew he could draw and fire before either of them could get their guns out, but he didn't. He wasn't sure just how bloody this pair was.

"Lost my watch here somewhere. I'm hunting it," Mark said.

"Sure, you are," the blond one said. "We'll help you find it." They came at him now, slowly from either side. Mark jumped to the clean, polished surface of the president's desk.

"You little boys shouldn't play a man's game," Mark said. "Run home to mother before you get hurt, Keith Zilke." Mark used one of the names from the Westerly list.

"Son of a bitch!" the smaller man said. "How the hell you know my name?"

"It don't matter none now," the blond said, grinning. "He ain't gonna be able to tell anybody your name or anything else."

"Is that so?" Mark said. "Joey Larson."

"How in hell . . . ?" The blond man stopped.

"I told you he was bad news, Wade. I told you you shouldn't snuff that agent guy."

75

"Shut up, dammit!" Wade screamed. He dug for something in his belt.

When the Penetrator saw the glint of a gun, his own .45 already in his hand, spoke sharply. The sound of the heavy cartridge going off shattered the silence of the room and deafened the men for a moment. The heavy lead slug caught Wade in the forehead, killing him instantly and driving his lifeless body backward against a file cabinet where it hung for a moment, before sliding down until he sat in nearly the same position Joey had. Wade's gun remained in his hand in a death grip.

Mark jumped down from the desk, his gun covering the smaller man.

"Zilke, do you want to die, too?"

Zilke was shaking so hard that he could barely stand up. His hand never went toward his belt. He moved his head from side to side, answering Mark as he stared at the body across the room.

"God, no, mister. The whole thing is his fault. He killed Joey just for fun. Said he hadn't had a real good kill in two years. He was crazy, that guy. He was just plain nuts."

"But you're smart, right, Zilke?"

"Yeah. I'm alive at least."

"You want to stay that way, don't you? Quickly, how did you know I was here?"

"Electronic sound detection stuff, pickups that radio any sound not programmed back to a central office. They heard you and sent us out."

"Anybody else coming?"

"No way. We always handle it."

"Who do you work for?"

"GTA."

"But this is Investments Unlimited."

76

"Same thing; all owned by the same guy."

"Who is that?"

"Some fat guy who always smokes a long cigar. A big shot, but I never heard his name."

"But you've been to his house on security matters?"

"Hell, no. He has somebody full time for that. He don't trust us that far."

"You work directly under Johnathan Westerly?"

"Sometimes. He's small fry."

"Did you break Melissa Martindale's arm?"

"Hell, no. Wade did that. I told you he enjoys that stuff."

"You push the Rolls over the cliff?"

Zilke began to get scared. He wasn't sure what to say.

"No. I wasn't even there. Wade did that, too."

"How far did the car drop?"

"I don't know."

"Why didn't you leave the key on and the motor running, when it went over?"

"Hell, we did. The motor was running. I told . . ." He stopped, but it was too late.

Mark slammed the bone-hard side of his hand into the crease of Zilke's neck, driving him to his knees, not breaking his neck, but almost knocking him out. Mark felt the anger rising in him, but he fought it down. He could not let raw anger dictate his actions. He must not. Mark helped Zilke to stand and walked him behind the desk, made him take pen and paper, sit down, and write a complete confession about his part in killing Brad Russell's date and breaking Melissa's arm. He claimed he didn't know anything about the death of the reporter. Mark believed him. That had been a specialist's job.

When Zilke signed the confession, the Penetrator

fastened his hands behind him and his feet together with black tape and taped him into the big chair. When Mark was sure the man couldn't move, the Penetrator vanished from the building the same way he had come in.

He stopped at a phone booth where he called homicide and reported a dead body in the building. He said there was also a confession to another murder. Mark hung up quickly and drove back to his motel. He was tired.

He still had to strip the barrel out of his .45 and dispose of it someplace where it never would be found. Mark carried a supply of new barrels in his suitcase.

The riflings on the death slug in Wade Kennedy's skull would never be matched. It was a little thing, a small precaution, but it was those little things that had kept the Penetrator alive and still fighting crime.

Chapter 8

BACKSTOPPING A POWER PLAY

The first thing Mark did when he woke up the next morning was dial his phone drop. A sleep-tinged voice answered.

"Good morning."

"Good morning. This is Ajax. Anything for me?"

"Who is it?"

"Ajax."

"Let's see. Oh, yes. Who killed you?"

"I killed myself because Achilles' armor was awarded to Odysseus."

"Right, you're Ajax. I have three identical messages for you, which came in late last night. All say: 'Please call L.L. That's L.L.' That's all. No number, no other messages."

"Thanks, and give my compliments to your chef."

"What?"

"Good-night, Gracie."

"Right."

He hung up and stared at the phone. L.L. That had to be Lorna Luna. What was on her mind? Three calls? She must have a tip that could be a good one. Something about GTA. They already represented her.

They bought up her contract when they gobbled up that first agency.

Mark dialed her private number and listened. It was the seventh ring before someone picked up the phone.

"Jeeeeeeez! Don't anybody ever answer the damn phone around here but me? Who's calling in the middle of the goddamned night?"

"Lorna, it's past seven-thirty."

"That's what I said, the middle of the fucking night. Who is this?"

"Lance Lansing. You called me three times last night."

"Oh, yeah, Lance, sweetheart." Her voice warmed considerably. "Dear, gorgeous boy, how are you? I had some trouble. I have in fact one damned big batch of trouble. GTA is on my back like a leech. They want me to help them talk Sinatra into signing with them. I say they're out of their minds. He does what he wants. And lordy, how he does it!"

"I can't help you any with that. I've never even met him."

"You can help me another way. GTA has sent a damn spy to watch me. He's out in front of my house right now in that damn black car. I'm staked out, for Christ's sake! And then they have this guy who keeps calling me. It's got so bad I don't even want to answer the phone."

Her voice was rising, and Mark could feel the anger, the fear, coming through. He gripped the instrument more tightly.

"Is there somebody in front of your house right now?"

"Lover boy, there sure as hell is. Now I figured it this way. You're looking for dirt on these creeps, right? So come over and nail this son of a bitch, and find out

80

what he's doing. Get him by the balls and twist them until he talks."

Mark grinned at the phone, remembering Lorna Luna and all the wild tales he'd heard about her salty language.

"Hey, hope you don't mind the way I talk. I sort of got in the habit. You can come out here, can't you?"

"Yes, of course. I'll be there in half an hour, maybe a little more depending on traffic. Don't let him inside your gate."

Mark hung up, dressed quickly in California casual, a pair of dark brown slacks, light tan shirt, open at the throat, and a sport coat. He left the shirt collar inside the coat.

The Penetrator drove out Santa Monica Boulevard into Beverly Hills to Ladyflower Lane, where he had been a few nights before. The gate to the mansion was open, and there was no guard. Mark drove in and parked. Lorna herself met him at the front door.

"Gorgeous boy! I'm so glad you could come." The star wore a heavy robe, with her initials in gold on one side. She had on her makeup, but a scarf covered her hair. Right then Lorna Luna looked more like a housewife than a star.

"Did you see him? There, just across from the drive on the other side. In that black car. He's been there for three hours now, and I'm afraid even to drive into the street. Chase him away for me, Lance. Please chase him away!"

Mark decided she was overplaying the part a little, but after all, she didn't have anybody writing this material for her.

"I'll go talk to him. You sure he isn't a cop? You know it isn't illegal to sit in your own car on a public street."

"It is in Beverly Hills. It's illegal to loiter on any residential street until you live there. Now go run him away. My hairdresser is coming soon."

Mark walked out the drive to the street and up behind the car. It was a new Lincoln Continental, black and beautiful. Mark palmed a hideout derringer from his pocket as he came up along the side of the car. The weapon was a High Standard .22 magnum derringer, compact and lightweight with two shots and a self-cocking action. He edged it over the open window in the driver's side door and pointed it at the man sitting behind the wheel.

"See this, hotshot? It's ready to blow two holes in your guts the size of a half dollar. Move over and keep quiet, but keep both hands in plain sight."

"What the hell?"

"Shut up and slide over. Watch the hands."

He was in his late twenties, soft, wearing a crumpled suit that looked as if it had been slept in. The man needed a shave. Mark guessed he was just under six feet, maybe two hundred pounds. His hair was cut in a flat-top, the first one Mark had seen in a long time. He looked straight out of a World War II movie. The driver wasn't more than twenty-five.

He slid over slowly, never taking his eyes off the two black muzzle holes of the twin-barreled derringer.

"Just take it easy with that piece, mac. I ain't going nowhere. Who are you?"

"I was about to ask you the same question. Are you watching Lorna Luna's house?"

"Yeah. So what?"

"Who told you to?"

"None of your business."

"This little piece makes it my business." Mark moved into the driver's seat, shifted the derringer to his left hand, and his right chopped down across the man's nose in a motion so quick he had no chance to avoid it. The hard side of Mark's hand peeled the skin off the punk's nose but didn't break it.

The man grunted in pain, blinked rapidly, and brought up his hand to his nose. He took a tissue from a box on the dash and stopped the bleeding.

"Now, hotshot, who do you work for?"

"Hell, you already know. GTA."

"That's Global Talent Agency?"

"Yeah."

"Why are you watching Miss Luna's house?"

He turned and looked out the window.

The key was in the ignition of the big car. Mark turned it on and started the engine. The flat-top turned, curious.

"We're driving to find a place a little less public, hotshot. I'm going to need to reason with you. I think my first appeal to your sense of fair play will be a .45 slug through your right kneecap. You'll never walk right again, but what the hell. It's a remarkably good way to loosen a tongue."

"You wouldn't do that."

"I damn sure will." Mark gunned the engine but didn't move the gearshift into drive. "Now why are you watching her place?"

"How the hell should I know? I'm a hired hand here, just like you. They say park out here until somebody relieves me. I park out here. They didn't tell me to watch for nothing. Not a damn thing. I don't even keep track of who comes and goes."

"Who gave you the orders?"

"Westerly."

"Is he the head of the whole security system for GTA?"

83

"I don't know. I work for him; that's *all* I know."

"How long have you been doing this for him?"

"Maybe six months now. Somebody else handles the rough stuff. They got a couple of creeps to do that."

"Correction. They used to have a couple of creeps." Mark stared at the man. He was sweating now, and he looked worried. Mark believed him about the mission. It was a fake stakeout? A phony. But why? Just to scare her? Probably. Mark patted down the man and found a .38 in shoulder leather. The Penetrator pushed the rounds out of the cylinder and threw the weapon and shells in the backseat.

"Hotshot, I'm giving you a break. Get this bucket of bolts out of here." Mark stepped from the car and closed the door. "You drive out of the area, and you stay away, understand, or I'll find you and chop you up for cat food. Then I'll blow your head off. Do you read me loud and clear?"

"Yeah, right. I hear you. Who the hell you working for, the rich, old broad inside?"

"No. I work for myself. Now drive, hotshot. Drive and don't look back."

Mark watched the big car move away quickly down the street, around the curve, and out of sight.

Lorna met Mark at the front door. She threw her arms around him and kissed his lips, then leaned back, grinning at him.

"God, I've wanted to do that ever since I saw you! He's gone. The damn car is gone. Darling, I don't know how to thank you."

"You just did."

"Oh, darling, but that's sweet!" Her smile faded as the phone rang. "Don't answer it. We'll let the maid get it. I don't know why they keep calling. I hardly know Mr. Sinatra. He wouldn't listen to anything I'd have to say anyway." The phone stopped ringing, and she seemed relieved.

"Last night was a terror. I've never been so frightened in my life. The doorbell rang once, and when we looked at the gate, there was no one there. Absolutely no one. It happened again about two o'clock this morning, and I woke up screaming. I really wanted to call the police last night. But I knew the tricksters would be gone. It's been harassment."

"Yes, you should have called the police. Your Beverly Hills force isn't tolerant of that kind of prank."

"And Chief Peterson is a personal friend. But I didn't want to get them involved. And then there's my health. Did you know I've taken two blood pressure pills and two of my nerve pills already today? I called the set and told them I simply can't come to work today. I'm still doing that TV movie, and they'll simply have to wait. They say it's costing them twenty thousand dollars an hour with me off the set. That's too bad. Oh, darling, would you check the front again and see if anyone is there?"

Mark walked to the gate and looked both ways. There wasn't a car parked along the street as far as he could see. That was real Beverly Hills class.

Back inside the house he told her the car hadn't come back.

"Thank God! Now maybe I can start putting myself back together." She turned away, and when she swung back toward him, she held a small caliber automatic in her hand, and it was pointed directly at Mark's stomach.

The Penetrator remained absolutely still. If it were a trap and she was any good, he was dead. But that meant she had to know what she was doing and could

85

actually pull the trigger. Then the corners of her mouth turned up, and she giggled.

"I never was convincing with guns, not even in *Murder In Chicago,* which was probably my only real gangster movie. They kept reshooting all the scenes where I had to use a gun. I'd either drop the gun or break up and ruin the shot."

She handed Mark the automatic barrel first. "Would you see what's wrong with this thing? It doesn't shoot or do anything. Somebody gave it to me months ago and told me to keep it loaded."

Mark relaxed as he accepted the weapon from her. It was a .32 automatic. He pulled the slide back, but no round ejected. The Penetrator pushed the magazine lock and let the magazine slip out of the handle.

"It isn't much of a problem, Miss Luna. Someone put the top round in the magazine backward. The slug tips downward, letting the slide ride over it, so it won't chamber."

"I imagine that's why it won't fire, which it doesn't. Can you fix it for me so it works right?"

Mark took the round out and reloaded it in the magazine, snapping it back into place in the handle. He pulled the slide, chambering a round, and put on the safety.

"Now it's ready to use. Just push off the safety here, aim, and fire."

"Yes, thanks, Lance. I don't know what I'd do around here without you."

"Now, about your security. You should keep your gate closed all the time. It isn't much, but it's something. Don't you usually have a guard on the gate?"

"No, just for parties."

"I suggest you hire a guard service to send you someone twenty-four hours a day for the next week.

86

Also get a man with two trained guard dogs to patrol inside the fence. Then go back to work at the studio, and forget about all this. Tell your producer that you demand a full-time, personal bodyguard whenever you're on the set. He should be glad to furnish you one."

"Yes, yes, what a smashing idea. You have a touch for the dramatic, Lance. Are you sure you're not an actor?"

"Sorry. Now I have an interview in a half hour. I'm going to have to leave. You call the people you need, and tell them to get out here within an hour. Besides that, don't you answer the phone anymore. That should take care of you for a few days."

She advanced on him, her arms outstretched. "Lance, darling, I don't know how I could have made it without you." She smiled her most seductive smile. "When you have some time, you might come back and see me. I think we'd get along just fine together."

She hugged him and kissed his cheek.

Mark grinned. "I'll make sure I do come back."

Ten minutes later he stopped at a phone booth and called the number Angie Perez had given him.

"Perez Investigations."

"Is this her answering service?"

"It certainly is."

"Can I leave a message?"

"Right. Shoot."

"Tell Angie this is Mark, and I want her to . . ."

"Sir, did you say Mark?"

"Yes."

"I have a request from her that you call her private number. It's 440-6644."

"Thanks."

He dialed the new number, and Angie answered.

"Hey, I've been waiting to hear from you. How can I help?"

She sounded sleepy, yet anxious. "First wake up. Then I want you to dig up all the background you can on Lorna Luna. I don't want her professional stuff. Just the dirt. The gossip. Who she worked for early in her career, who she slept with back then, who she fought with, who she borrowed money from. Go back fifteen or twenty years."

"And you want it all in an hour, right, Mark?"

"No, take all morning. I'll give you a call about one."

"Yes, sir. I can do that." She paused and Mark waited.

"Hey, do you like good Mexican food?"

"I love it. Why?"

"Just wondered. I'll give you a call about your little girl friend, Lorna Luna, as soon as I can."

She hung up and Mark Hardin smiled.

Chapter 9

SLOW DISSOLVE TO REALITY

Jeffrey Scott Duncann leaned back in his executive, leather desk chair and examined the chipped, blue-flint arrowhead that had just been delivered to him. Curious, he thought. It looked authentic, as if some Indian had chipped the flint off in small flakes with a stone to form the sharp point. He had been something of a Western expert and hobbyist in his younger days, and now with the help of a magnifying glass, he was sure the arrowhead was a real one, and it looked hand chipped.

"Yes," he said half out loud. "Genuine, no doubt at all. Either Sioux or perhaps Cheyenne." The heavy-set man shook his head in confusion. What in the world was an Indian arrowhead doing on Westerly's desk? It didn't make sense. But the more he thought about it the more he remembered an old newspaper story. It was about a do-gooder, part Indian, who had developed a career for himself charging around the country battling against all the bad guys he could find. Some strange name they had given him . . . yes, the Penetrator. He had built up quite a reputation for showing up in crisis situations and bashing in a few heads and winning the day for the good guys.

J.S. let his eyes go wide in surprise. Here? The Penetrator was interested in this little scam? Impossible. It had to be a trick that Westerly was playing on him. But Westerly was as frightened as a man could be. He wasn't faking it. He must have met this Penetrator face to face. At least he had lived to talk about it. Most people didn't.

This had to be kept quiet. J.S. did not want the press to pick up the story, or it would be blown all out of proportion and GTA would suffer. No, he had to keep this arrowhead thing all quiet and confidential, even top secret.

Unfortunately, this Penetrator wasn't the kind of man you could call up and bribe, or even reason with. In fact, nobody knew who he was or where he lived. He just turned up where the trouble was. So how did he happen to land in Hollywood? Oh, hell! The damn broken arm, the Rolls over the cliff, and the newspaper reporter spread all over the freeway. The violence had drawn him to Hollywood the way blood in the ocean pulls in sharks from miles around. It must be the same genuine killer instinct.

J.S. allowed himself the luxury of a quick shudder before he moved into action. He called Westerly and chewed him out for two minutes. "It all boils down to the simple idea that we can't afford any more violence. Do you understand that, Westerly?"

"Yes, sir. But that's going to make some areas much more difficult."

"That's tough. We're almost there. Slow down a little if you need to. We need another dozen stars, top names, and we'll be ready to make our move."

He was off and flying; he had it working in his mind, and he couldn't stop.

"I've rented this big place down the street here in

Beverly Hills. It's been vacant in an estate hassle, and somebody went in there to make a horror film. I've rented it with all the special effects still in place. It should be a lulu of a setup for our big announcement party. It's one hell of a nice latchup."

J.S. cut off abruptly and didn't say a word. He was thinking. Westerly sat at his end of the line patiently waiting. He knew the boss had changed directions or was thinking something through.

"Get up here, Westerly. We'll have a late breakfast. I want to go over something with you in person. Leave there right now. Any questions?"

"No, sir, J.S. I'll be right over."

Twenty-nine minutes later Westerly walked into the big office in J.S. Duncann's home, where he conducted all his business. It was a montage shot of dozens of his big productions, with trophies, photographs, film cans, pictures on the walls, parts of sets—to any nonmovie buff it might seem more like a junk yard than a working office. Duncann sat there for a moment looking at his treasures, ignoring Westerly. He saw the longhorn steer horns from a charging range cow that almost ran down his camera car on *The Rawhiders,* the fez from *Desert Battle Plan,* and the silver skates given to him by the darling of the ice extravaganzas of the 1930s.

Now Hollywood told him to pack it all in, to forget he was one of the greatest producers of all time. They told him to walk away, to lie down, put his face in the dust, and die.

Well, he would fool the lot of them. He wasn't sure just how he would do it yet. Would he make a grandiose announcement? Should he tell them the power that he had over them and dare them to challenge him?

Or would it be more satisfying to work in the background as the best producers always do, pulling strings, making people jump to his unseen commands, to guide one after the other of the biggest studios into bankruptcy? He was still considering it. If he took them on one at a time, it would be six months or a year before anyone realized what was happening. By then it would be too late. He could nip them off individually, buy up the dregs, and really put together a fantastic production company. If there were only time. He knew he wasn't young anymore. He accepted the fact and lived with it. He knew he could do a quick and final fade-out at anytime. But he tried not to think about that . . . he had to think positively again.

J.S. put down the script he was reading and looked up at Westerly.

"Well, don't just stand there. Sit down."

"We have some problems?"

Jeffrey Scott Duncann scowled at Westerly. Damn, he wanted a cigar. The stupid doctor had told him no more stogies. "Christ, Westerly, why are you always trouble for me? I gave you the whole agency business to play with, and you continue to fuck it up. Now we've got this guy called the Penetrator on our backs."

"Who? I don't understand."

"You never understand, Westerly. That guy who scared you in your office. He wasn't really there as an actor. He was the bastard they call the Penetrator. You and your dynamite bomb on that reporter's car probably brought him here. Now he's sniffing around where we don't want him. He's a self-styled crime fighter, and he doesn't mind working the wrong side of the law."

"Don't remind me about that man," Westerly said. "He's deadly, like a rattlesnake all coiled and ready to strike from a foot away, and there's nothing you can do to stop it."

"Well, sonny-boy, now's your chance to stop him.

You can protect yourself—and me, too. I want you to do a job on him. Snuff him. Call in your little Italian friends—no, let me do it. I have some muscle I haven't used in a long time. I don't want this Penetrator snooping around anymore."

"But you said no more violence."

"That was with the stars, dumbshit."

"Oh, now we get the Penetrator."

"Yes, Westerly. The Penetrator. You've got a press party set for tonight after shooting out at Universal for that new jiggle girl you're promoting?"

"Yes, Wendy Tyler, and she is something. Going to be very big."

"So all we have to do is arrange for the Penetrator to know about the party and get him out there. You've publicized it right, I hope, so the media will be there and lots of others will show up as well?"

"Right, Mr. Duncann. We did a special PR job on this because the jiggle girls are really big right now, and we can get a lot of good exposure on Wendy."

"You hit all the newspapers, the TV folks, even radio? Now we need to get some consumer stuff, maybe call the radio news guys, or the TV news, so we can get something on today. We want this joker to hear about it. Bring out the fact that all of the GTA big brass will be there to show support for Wendy. Try to get that in hard, so this joker will come out there to see us, maybe to talk to us or threaten or something. We want to get him on our turf so we can do a job on him."

"But it's set up for tonight at eight-thirty. That doesn't give us much time."

"Right, Westerly. Use your inside contacts. Tell the radio and TV you really need a favor to get some good PR on the five o'clock news. Radio can go anytime.

Hit that all-news show hard. We need this spread as fast as we can." Duncann paused for a minute. "Why the hell are you standing there, Westerly? Get out of here, and get busy calling the press. Put a dozen people on it if you have to."

"Yes, sir. We'll sure try. That's a tough one."

"Don't give me that bullshit. Just get out of here, and get the job done."

Westerly gulped twice, turned, and went out to try to do what he considered an impossible job.

Duncann watched him go. He wasn't sure why he put up with the bastard. Oh, he was good at his trade. Duncann had picked him up with the first agency GTA bought.

Then Duncann forgot Westerly. He concentrated on the Penetrator. Knowing what he did about the man, Duncann was concerned. It was only a fifty-fifty chance that the Penetrator would hear about the party. But if he did, Duncann would have some special friends there to meet him. He'd take care of those arrangements personally so he was sure it would be done right.

His glance settled on a bald eagle as it had been frozen in landing. The statue decorated one end of the wall of his office. The bird had a four-foot wingspread and had been used in *Eagles Never Die,* his epic air force film that he hoped would be a classic. Already it had grossed over forty million and was still climbing.

Duncann looked away from the eagle. It had been his favorite symbol. Now if he were going to have any chance to fly again, he had to clear up this current unpleasantness and get his production company back on the road. He wanted to make a sequel to the space picture so bad he could think of little else. J.S. had read three scripts for it already and had another one lined up. At least the writers hadn't blackballed him.

He looked back at the script, and his eyes widened for a moment. Then he settled down to read the rest of the story. He would lick the bastards. Hollywood couldn't keep him down forever! He'd beat them at their own blacklisting game!

Chapter 10

KEYSTONE KOPS, REAL BULLETS

It was late afternoon when Mark went back to his motel and dropped on the bed, needing an hour's sleep. He told himself he would wake up promptly at six o'clock and go have dinner. He woke as he had ordered himself to do, remembered his telephone drop, and called the number. There was a message for him to call Angie at home. Mark dialed her number and heard it ring twice before Angie caught it and said hello.

"This is Mark. You called?"

"Yes, I thought you might be interested in this. GTA is making a big deal about a rather routine thing tonight. They have invited the press and a few guests to Universal Studios to meet, interview, and take pictures of one of their new little jiggle girls."

"Wait a minute. What's a jiggle girl?"

"You don't know? You just haven't heard that term. The filmmakers take a pretty girl with big boobs and put her in a tight blouse or a sweater with no bra, or a nothing bra, and let her run around through the plot. Without even trying, the poor dear jiggles her boobs all over the place, and the men in the TV audience just sit there and call for more. Those are the 'jiggle girls.' "

"You're right. I have noticed them," Mark said.

"I bet. Anyway, GTA has a new one they're promoting, and they're having a champagne party for her after work wraps on the set tonight at Universal. The strange part is they sent out their normal PR on the bash a week ago. Now, this afternoon, they're flooding the radio, TV news, and print media with special invitations, reminders, and personal calls for people to be there. Then they add one item. They say tonight GTA will make an important announcement about how it will be involved with its clients and the industry in the future."

"What's so unusual about all that?"

"It isn't that big a story. The little jiggle girl is a nobody, and they give these promo parties every month or so. They have emphasized to everyone that tonight all the big brass from Global will be here. It's highly unusual for an agency to push itself forward this way and especially at the last minute at an already scheduled promotion. Something is out of whack."

"You're saying it could smell like a trap?"

"I'm not sure," Angie said. "Are they aware that we're investigating them? How much do they know about you? Why would they want to get a lot of their brass at a deal like this? Are they trying to get somebody besides the press to show up? Like maybe you? And why would they do that?"

"The why is easy. They know I'm after them. I left my Senate calling card on a desk a couple of days ago. Why they would want me out there is easy. It's their turf. It's their home country where they should be able to rig the situation in their favor. I agree it does sound fishy, maybe a trap, and that's why you can't go. I'll go out and see what's going on. Can you get me through the front gate?"

"I can, but the pass is for two journalists."

"Easy. It will work for one just fine," Mark said and paused. "No argument from you?"

"You'll find that I'm not the arguing type."

He made arrangements to pick up the press pass from her and then dressed for the show. He drove to Universal, just beyond Hollywood, and got there an hour before the event was set to start. Inside the studio he walked around awhile with his small briefcase, then slid into an open door at a vacant sound stage and quickly took out a pair of carpenter's coveralls from the briefcase. He pulled them on over his three-piece suit and put on a cloth painter's cap, discarding the briefcase. Mark made certain that all of his weapons were safe and not noticeable. Then he walked around until he found the right sound stage, number nine, and went in through a small door.

Already there were people scurrying about. A caterer worked setting up three tables behind a screen and loading them with both hot and cold hors d'oeuvres. Mark found a four-foot piece of two-by-two and carried it to the far side of the big barn-like building. It looked like a huge airplane hangar, with a thirty-foot-high ceiling and no support beams anywhere. The ceiling and walls were all covered with foot-thick bats of soundproofing and insulation, evidently to keep away all the outside sounds. Up near the roof were catwalks, and in some areas over sets, many long pipes hung from cables to the ceiling. Each pipe had dozens of various-sized lights, all aimed at the set.

Mark knew just enough about a movie set to be interested in it all without getting totally lost. They were through shooting for the day on the one live set, and the director was replacing some lighting and doing a

98

run through of a small bit on an interior set. Mark had no idea of what the show might be. He stayed far enough away so no one would wonder why he was there or ask him to do something that he probably wouldn't know how to do anyway. The Penetrator found an old set close by and moved behind it where he could still see what was happening, but where no one could see him.

The champagne arrived and was displayed near the hot and cold food. It was plain the rehearsal set was where the jiggle girl would be, or perhaps she was there already. Mark waited. The rest of the huge sound stage was dark now, except for a path of lights from the main door to the set. People and equipment began arriving. Mark saw three different Los Angeles TV stations represented, with directors, technicians, mini-cameras, and the on-the-spot reporters. He saw cables extending out to TV sound trucks to relay the picture to the station.

By the time of the press preview, there were fifty journalists in the big set area, sampling the champagne and the food.

Mark discarded his coveralls and painter's cap and mingled with the media people. He had on his three-piece brown suit to blend in with the other news types and felt right at home. Mark held a plastic glass of champagne as he circulated but saw neither of the two GTA people he had identified before, Johnathan Westerly or the man at Lorna's party he had sent the note to. The Penetrator kept moving, and he hoped that Westerly was not there watching for him from behind another set somewhere. Soon Mark saw one show biz reporter from a TV station and another longtime TV anchor man.

Three Keystone Kops in full costume circulated

through the party, making believe they were arresting people and trying pratfalls that didn't seem to come off. Mark couldn't understand them. They were neither actors nor stunt men.

Across the room Mark thought he saw a familiar face. It was only a flash, but he kept track of the girl and soon worked his way near her. She turned and grinned at him with deep brown eyes.

"Hi, Mark!" It was Angie Perez with large horn-rimmed glasses, a clipboard, and pen. She was playing script girl from another set. The clipboard she carried had printed on the first page in large block letters: CALL SHEET.

"Don't look so angry and concerned, Mark. I told you I'm not the type to argue."

"You just go ahead and do whatever you want to."

"Only when I think I can help. See the man in the pink coat and the brown pants by the champagne table? He's the third man in the GTA organization. He was introduced to me one time as the controller of GTA. That means the money man."

"You know any others around here? What about Westerly? Have you seen him?"

"I don't know him. He's the head talent man. Wasn't he the one who interviewed you?"

"True. Now get lost and stay out of trouble. I don't want anybody to make a connection between us."

She smiled, leaned up, and kissed his cheek. "Darling, it's good to see you again, too. Bye bye." She winked and moved away through the growing crowd.

The jiggle girl came out ten minutes later, was announced by Westerly, and given a chance to say a few words before the press began asking her questions. The bright lights came on, and the TV people moved in with mikes and cameras for their interviews. She jiggled this way and that way and gave the cameramen a lot of footage that would never be permitted on family television news broadcasts. Mark faded away from the bright lights and put some distance between him and Westerly. He didn't want the GTA man to recognize him. Mark wished he had some kind of a minimum disguise.

A minute later Westerly came on with the big announcement from GTA about the new direction they were taking. It seemed like nothing new to Mark. Simply the idea that GTA was going to try to exercise more control over the type of parts their stars took in order to guide and direct their clients into better and better pictures to ensure that their careers would steadily progress.

The more Mark thought about it the more certain he was that the whole "big announcement" had been a last minute try at some publicity. Either that or a ploy to help get Mark on the lot.

Mark spotted another man wearing a large blue-and-white GTA badge and a second round one in yellow that said, "ASK ME!" The Penetrator went up to him and grinned.

"Lordy, lordy, can you tell me what those twin beauties measure with the old tape?"

"Yes, sir. She's a natural thirty-eight incher, and that's without any silicone transplants. She's a natural wonder."

"Lordy, lordy, now that's something to write home to my editor about."

"Yes, we certainly hope that you do that, sir."

Mark moved on, looking for a GTA man who might know something important about the organization. The Keystone Kops captured the jiggle girl and carried her off, then brought her back, and did it again for the TV cameras. Mark searched for a GTA man he could have a quiet little chat with over in the dark section of the big sound stage.

The interviews were over, and the TV crews had left by the time Mark found the man he wanted. He had a large blue-and-white GTA badge, as well as a name tag, and under it the title of executive vice president. The Penetrator asked a question and worked the man to one side. They chatted a minute, and the party was over. The caterers swept in and took out the last of the goodies, and the news types vanished out the front door.

"What network were you with again?" the GTA man asked.

"CBC, Canadian Broadcasting Company. The same one you're with."

"What do you mean by that?"

Mark saw the bulge under the man's coat. It had to be a gun.

Mark put his arm around the man and walked him toward the darkness. "Now don't give me a bad time, or I'll twist this arm right off. You understand that?"

"Yes, but what's going on?"

"You aren't with GTA. I know all of the big shots. Who are you, and what are you doing here?"

The man tried to break free. He was surprisingly strong. Mark grabbed an arm, pulled it behind the man, and twisted the hand toward his neck. He walked the man into the darkness away from the lighted set.

"Over here, Goddammit!" The man Mark held yelled. "This is the one, over here behind the set!"

Mark heard feet pounding behind him. He spun around with his captive. Three men charged from the shadows into the small pool of light. They were the three Keystone Kops, but now each carried a nightstick in one hand and a thirty-inch short sword in the other. They looked like they knew how to use their weapons.

Mark stripped the gun from the man he held, and pushed him to the floor out of the way. Mark whirled, moved with his back against the set, and looked at the men coming at him. He drew Ava and remembered he had only sleep darts in it, six of them. Now he aimed the .38 he'd gotten from the friendly vice president at one thug and Ava at a second one.

"You're all dead if you keep coming. Why not just back off and stay alive?" The Keystone Kops hesitated but came closer.

"Get him, you gutless bastards!" the man on the floor shouted. "What do you think I'm paying you for!"

They advanced again, one on each side, one directly ahead.

Ava was Mark's silent weapon, now loaded with darts that pumped a combination of sodium pentothal and M-99 tranquilizer directly into the bloodstream or tissue. Mixed in with the tranquilizer was a load of a secret muscle-spasming agent. The instant the fluid hit the tissue, it shocked the muscular system, causing most voluntary muscles to cramp and spasm uncontrollably. This effectively put a victim down as well as a .45 slug in his head. Once hit with a tranquilizer with the spasming agent, the target had approximately a tenth of a second to react before he lost all control of his arms and legs.

Mark shot the closest Keystone Kop in the chest. He yelped in surprise and started to touch his shirt when the spasming hit him, and he shook like a man with a jackhammer, twitching arms and legs. He dropped his sword and baton and melted to the floor on the spot.

Mark shot the second Keystone Kop in the shoulder

and then had to dodge to one side as the third slashed at him with the saber, cut through the painted cotton muslin of the flat behind him and crashed through. Mark ran the other way. By now Mark had put Ava away, and he took out his Detonics .45 pistol.

Two more men jumped into the area across from the set. One drew down on Mark with a handgun that went off just as Mark dove past the edge of a tree. Too late Mark discovered the tree was only a shell of fiber glass and chicken wire. The slug ripped through the fiber glass as Mark squirmed into a bathroom set and out the back where he got to his feet.

Mark sprinted for the darkest part of the huge sound stage. He heard shouts behind him and heavy boots pounding the concrete floor. As he ran, he worked up his night sight with his *Sho-tu-ça*. By the time he found the wall, he was deep into unused sets, a pair of houses, and a plywood Sherman tank. By then the Penetrator realized he had instinctively headed for the dark and probably had trapped himself. In doing so he had angled for the corner of the building—and the only one without a doorway. The Penetrator spotted a wooden ladder against the wall ahead and ran silently for it, slipped the pistol back into its shoulder home, and climbed the ladder without the whisper of a noise.

Once above the level of the sets, Mark stopped climbing and looked around. No one remained at the jiggle-girl set. The lights had even been killed there. There were only Mark, the Keystone Kops, and at least two other bad guys. Mark climbed another five rungs and stepped on a catwalk that swung on cables twenty feet over the sound stage floor. It was three feet wide, and it swayed as Mark moved out on it. Fifteen feet from the wall, the Penetrator lay down on the catwalk and looked over the side. He saw one of the men below him working towards the ladder. Mark drew silent Ava and fired the CO-2-powered weapon twice. One of the darts hit flesh, and the man gave a hoarse cry before his muscles began twitching and he pitched to the floor.

Mark had no idea how many hunters there were left below. Two at least. He worked slowly along the catwalk. Soon it began to sway and creak. Mark stopped moving. He could see a larger area, almost all of the sound stage. If they didn't suddenly turn on the lights, he would be in a perfect position. He had the high ground, always a prized military objective for the foot soldier.

Without warning, a shot from below ripped through a board near his feet. Mark pulled his legs up and waited, trying to see where the flash came from. Another shot boomed—he spotted the gunman, and the round missed. Before Mark could fire at the position, a heavy boom came from below, and Mark knew it was a .45 sounding off. No lead came anywhere near him. From below he heard a groan, and the man who had fired at Mark ran for the far side of the stage. The small door slammed, and all was quiet in the building.

A moment later a voice came from near the dark set directly below.

"I know where you are now, man. You get your ass down here, or I'll blast you so full of holes you'll think you're a screen door."

Mark saw the new gunman, kneeling between a pair of stored flats. He was looking upward at the catwalk. Mark dug out a golf-ball-like object from his pocket. It was white and looked like a golf ball, but in reality it was a small tear gas bomb, pressure-filled with compressed nausea and tear gas. Mark threw it downward. It hit on a two-by-four set piece and showered gas onto the man as the frangible shell of the ball broke. The gunman ran away from the gas. Mark got up and hurried back along the catwalk to the ladder and went silently down it.

A few moments later the voice came again. "Nice try, but it didn't work. If that had been nerve gas, I'd be dead. But I know about tear gas. Now I'm going to tear you apart!"

Mark could not locate the voice. He used his ultrasensitive hearing to catalog all movements in the sound stage. He heard only two individuals. One directly ahead and one to the left. He moved toward the closest one ahead. The person was coming toward Mark. The Penetrator waited just inside the door of a living room set. The finished section was in front of him and the false part, the backstage section, behind. The other person was on the edge of the finished side of the living room set and coming forward. Mark could see him now, a shadow that slid behind a large sofa, slithered along behind it, lifted up and looked around, and crawled again in back of a big chair. The crawler worked around the chair and eyed the open door. Mark let him get almost to the door, then jumped in front of the man, who was still flat on his stomach.

Mark kicked him in the side, saw the surprise on the man's face, and saw his right hand come up with a gun in it. Before the man could shoot, and before Mark could kick the gun away, a shot came from off the set. The man's hand flew backwards, his gun falling out of the suddenly useless fingers.

Mark kicked the weapon away and dodged behind the heavy upholstered chair. For a moment he had forgotten about the other movement he had heard.

"That should be the last one," a woman's voice said.

"Angie?" Mark asked.

106

"You were expecting maybe Wonder Woman or at least that bionic type who is as strong as a bulldozer?"

Mark chuckled. "You sure that's the last one?"

"According to my count. I've always been a good counter up to six, and that's all I saw join in the fun."

"Wait a minute," Mark said. They both were quiet for what Mark counted out as two minutes. The only sounds were the sobbing and moans of the man in front of Mark.

At last Mark moved and propped the man against the living room couch and looked at his wounded arm.

"You'll live, if you talk fast enough so you don't bleed to death. Who do you work for?"

"GTA."

"Who else do you work for?"

"Nobody."

"Who assigned you to gun me down?"

"None of your damned business."

"I just made it my business."

Before anything more could be said, the main overhead lights in the entire sound stage nine came on all at once. Mark's *Sho-tu-ça* dilated eyes went blind as the nearly sunshine intensity of the light hit them. He felt Angie's hand grab his, and they were running. Gradually his eyes adapted to the new brilliance, closing down his dilated pupils until he could see a little.

Angie led him past one set, around another, and to a small door in the wall. They went through the door and into the coolness of the Universal Studios street. They were between deserted sound stages, and they leaned against the wall, catching their breath. Both put away their weapons and began to walk towards the main studio gate.

Mark looked down at her. "How in the world did you know about that small door?"

"I saw it while we were walking around, before the people left and the shooting started. I asked somebody what it was for. Some wiseacre told me it was the midget's entrance. He was kidding, but the door sure worked."

The frown remained on Mark's face. "How many rounds did you fire back there?"

"Two."

"Then you hit that last guy in the arm and the goon who shot at me when I was on the catwalk. Out of two shots in the dark you made two hits."

"So?"

"So thanks. It could have been a bit messy for me back there without you."

"You would have made it fine. I was just showing off. But since I was there, I thought I might as well help."

"Want to get rid of the incriminating barrel of that .45 of yours?"

She smiled. "I've heard of doing that, but I never really had any reason to before."

"Do you now?"

"No, I don't think so. Those two will never file a police report about being shot. Anyway, a wrist wound won't hold a slug. They probably never will find that one. My guess is the slug wound up in a set or a flat or maybe in that insulation on the wall."

They had been cleared by the night guard and were at the parking lot for visitors. Mark stood beside his rented car.

"Thanks again for the help," he said. "I usually work alone, but you came in rather handy back there. You get anything on our friend, Luna?"

"A whole batch. Some of it that may surprise you. If you buy me a pizza, I'll tell you all."

"I don't suppose you know a place around here that sells good pizza?" Mark laughed. "I shouldn't have asked. I'm sure you know one, so lead on in your car and I'll follow."

She did.

Chapter 11

QUICK CUT TO DANGER

Just before they drove out of the Universal Studios parking lot, Angie pulled her Fiesta over, stopped, and ran back to where Mark had driven in behind her car.

"I know a lot better place to have pizza than any of them around here," she said. "It's back in Hollywood, so just follow me." She grinned, didn't give him a chance to say anything, ran back to her all-red Fiesta, and drove away.

Twenty minutes later she pulled up in front of a twelve-unit condominium just a few blocks off Wilshire. She was out of her car quickly, locking it, and walking back to Mark's rig.

"You guessed it; this is my place. I make a tremendous pizza. Just wait until you taste it."

Mark scowled at her and shook his head. "I still think you must be part Italian."

She laughed and caught his arm and led him up the steps to her third-floor unit.

"There's an elevator, but I needed the hike," she said, flashing brown eyes at him with just a hint of a grin.

Her condo was a one-bedroom without a view. The gold-and-brown carpet was reflected in the colors used in draperies and in the long couch and chair in the living room. The walls held modern paintings, mostly large and without frames. Mark had the idea she knew the artists.

The whole place was neat and orderly, much like its owner, he decided. A small kitchen had brown built-in stove top, oven, and refrigerator to go with matching antiqued cabinets.

"I bought this place because it had lots of drawers and cupboards in the kitchen. When I was growing up, Mother never had enough cabinets for things."

Mark wandered into the living room and saw a jigsaw puzzle half finished on a card table. It was a picture of a huge banana split and titled, "Dieter's Delight."

"This room looks like you, Angie. Did you decorate it?"

She came in wiping her hands on a towel and nodded. "Yes, I kind of threw it together."

"No. You don't throw things together. You're neat and precise but with a wild streak in you that leads to insubordination. I also like the great way you show off those pants and that blouse."

"Hey, you noticed. I think you just won an extra piece of pizza—the part without sausage."

Ten minutes later she had the crust of the pizza made and flattened out in a ten-inch pan. Then she put in the sauce and the cheese topping. She added pepperoni, mushrooms and sausage.

He watched her. "You mean someone actually eats things like that?"

"It's the old Italian style. My old Italian grandmother taught me how one day in Sicily. Now why don't I tell you what I dug up on the sweetheart of American flicks, the great and loved Lorna Luna."

111

"Good news, I hope. I could use some."

"Lorna is quite a girl. I mean, she invented the idea of swinging before the word was thought of. She came to Hollywood when she was seventeen and began making the rounds. She slept with everybody she thought might help her get a part or an agent. By the time she was twenty-one she had outlasted half the other sweet young things and had slept her way to more than a dozen small roles in movies.

"None of this hurt her career, and because she did have a natural talent, she began moving up in the business to better pictures. She was a top star by the time she was twenty-five. There's no way to list all of the names she was associated with romantically in those early days without writing a Who's Who of Hollywood. The gossip columnists of the Los Angeles papers finally got tired of talking about her bed hopping, and the only time she was mentioned was when she lasted more than a month with any one man. That made news.

"From what I can find out lately, she has done an about face and is now more interested in helping young actresses with their careers. She also has taken to sleeping with the nudie cuties, and this has turned some of her old friends against her. But she's still a star, still commands huge prices for her films, and has all the work she wants.

"She was with that first small agency, and GTA bought her contract early, but it doesn't seem like she's having any trouble with them."

"Who did she make the most pictures for?" Mark asked.

"Oh, let's see." Angie flipped through her notes. "She made twelve features for Duncann Productions. That's the same outfit that did *Starbound Space War*, the big winner this year that's launching a whole raft of science fiction movies. But Duncann hasn't done anything since."

"Not much help there. I can't figure her out. She says GTA is putting pressure on her to get her to talk Sinatra into signing with them. She says she hardly knows the man."

Angie flipped her note pages again. "She knew him very well when he was in his last year with the Hit Parade. For about three months they were never apart."

"She says she can't even get to talk to him now."

Angie looked at her watch. "Pizza in twelve minutes. Want to help me set the table?"

They set it, and Angie made tossed green salad with half a tomato on each one and vinegar-and-oil dressing.

"So where are we?" Angie asked. "How close are we to anything that would stand up in court?"

"Nowhere. We haven't got a damn thing. One confession that I know the DA wouldn't even listen to. The guy will claim duress and scream his head off. Oh, did you see anything in the papers about a guy being arrested in the Investments Unlimited offices?"

"Sure did. Turned out there was another guy there with a bullet in his forehead, and he was dead. The other one was alive, and he's yelling to the DA about some mystery man who tied him up with tape, killed his friend, and ran out. The person described sounds a lot like you."

"There was nothing about a confession? Nothing about Brad Russell's girl friend who was killed in his Rolls Royce?"

"Not a word about that."

"Figures."

113

Mark picked up Angie's phone and dialed his drop. There was only one message. It asked him to call L.L. at once.

Mark put down the phone and watched Angie checking on the pizza. "That was our friendly star, Lorna Luna, who wants me to call her at once."

"What about?"

"I don't know; probably another crisis."

"Don't call before pizza. It'll be ready now in exactly two minutes, and this one you've got to get while it's hot."

Mark could smell the cooking pizza. "Her crisis is going to wait."

A half hour later when the pizza was gone, the salad devoured, and the beer drained, Mark called Lorna Luna's private number.

The phone rang ten times. Mark waited. Two more rings at last brought an answer.

"Yeah, what you want?" It was a deep, heavy voice.

"Is Lorna there."

"Yeah, but she can't come to the phone now."

"She called me and needs to talk to me."

"Nope, she can't do that."

"Would you tell her this is Lance Lansing, and I want to talk to her?"

"Hell, no, I won't do that."

The receiver on the other end of the line slammed down hard. Mark sat there looking at the instrument.

"Well, the goons have taken over her house, it seems. I've got to get out there. Some nerd answered and said Lorna couldn't come to the phone."

"You mean they kidnapped her?"

"I don't know. Last time I left there I gave her enough security to guard a president."

"But I thought you said she had already signed with GTA."

"This is another hassle." He stood. "Thanks for the pizza and the company. And you thank your Italian grandmother for me." He bent to kiss her cheek, and she let him.

"I'll tell the old dear. Her Italian name is Lupe Cervantes."

They both laughed.

Before he went out the front door, Mark checked his weapons. He'd get another load of darts for Ava from his arms suitcase in the trunk of the car.

Mark hesitated at the door. "Oh, if you don't have anything else to do, see if you can track down who owns these phone numbers. One of them is GTA. I don't know who belong to the other three." He recited the numbers he had memorized in the GTA offices, and she wrote them down. "Those could be important, but I don't know how just yet."

"I'll give you a call tomorrow," Angie said.

He waved and ran for the car.

Thirty-five minutes later, Mark stopped half a block from the Lorna Luna mansion and looked over the scene. Nothing seemed out of place. The gates were open, but maybe she expected someone. Mark adjusted his hardware and walked down the street, through the gate, and up to the front door. Where was the security? No guard at the gate, the gate open, and no guard dogs. He pushed the bell, and at once the door swung open. A maid in uniform stood there, smiling nervously.

"Yes, sir?" she asked.

"I'm Lance Lansing. Miss Luna called me."

"Oh, yes, right this way. Go down the hall and to the second door on the right." She pointed the way, stepped aside, and looked back at him once as she walked quickly into the living room. Mark frowned at her and took half a dozen steps down the hall.

It had happened before to him, that special sense of danger. The first time had been on a muddy road in Vietnam when he was leading a squad on a recon patrol. It was as still as death with the high grass on all sides. Suddenly he knew it was a trap.

"Hit the ditch, now!" he had screamed, and the eight men dove into the protection of the ditch two seconds before vietcong automatic weapons opened up from ambush.

Now Mark had the same creepy, crawly feeling along the back of his neck. He took two more steps down the ornate hallway before he lunged to one side behind a marble pillar.

At that exact moment two automatics blasted hot lead at him from both sides of the hall.

Chapter 12

CLOSE-UP SHOT, NUDIE SCENE

Mark's .45 came into his hand as he dove for the marble pillar after some sixth-sense warning, and the shots blasted from down the hall. He turned and looked behind him. Keith Zilke, the same man Mark had taped to a chair in the investments building and who had signed a confession, was sighting down on Mark with a long-barreled revolver. Mark rolled, snapped off a shot, and saw Zilke take the round in the throat and jolt backwards to the floor, his hands clutching at his throat, trying to stop the gushing blood. His eyes were angry, terrified, as he stared at Mark. Zilke knew he was dying.

There were no more shots from in front of Mark now, so he stormed toward the first door in the hallway. The Penetrator ran through the open doorway fast at an angle in the best police style and came up empty-handed. It was a small sewing room, with an old-fashioned quilting frame along one wall with a quilt in work. Someone had been stitching over the double wedding-ring pattern, a highly difficult and painstaking job. Mark couldn't stop to admire it. He stepped across the hall and checked the other room. A shot smashed into the doorframe at eye level as Mark crouched and looked around. Someone went out the window. Mark charged into the other room, the .45 in his right hand and Ava in his left. The room, set up for conferences with a polished cherry-wood table in the center, was now empty. Mark looked out the side of the window into the back lawn. He saw a man running past the lights near the swimming pool.

Mark kicked through the window, jumped to the ground, and ran after him. One shot came at Mark but went wide. The man ahead was small and moved like an experienced runner. The Penetrator had one chancy shot as the man was backlighted by the floodlights on the lawn, but he missed. Mark sprinted at an angle to the man's path, cut him off, and forced him back towards the house.

Once his target was on the level lawn again, he came into the glare of the floodlights. Mark aimed low and fired three quick shots. One cut through the calf of the runner's leg and sent him sprawling on the lawn and snarling in pain.

Mark crawled behind a large eucalyptus tree for cover.

"Throw away your gun," Mark said.

Instead the man lifted it and aimed the revolver at the tree.

"Drop it or you die on the spot. Is it worth that?"

The man threw the weapon onto the grass.

"Now get over here and bandage up this leg before I bleed to death," the wounded man said.

Mark picked up the .38 revolver, pushed it in his belt, and frisked the man quickly. He had no other weapon.

"Who else is inside? Where is Lorna Luna?"

"Why should I tell you? Fix my leg first."

Mark slapped him gently and held his face by the jaw.

"You're still alive; be thankful for that. Do you want to push your luck and try for dead? How many men inside?"

"Just three of us all together. Damn, that leg hurts."

Mark ran hard for the rear door of the big house and slid inside without a sound.

Screaming came from above. Mark rushed up the main staircase with both guns out as if he were assaulting an enemy position. He found no one in the hallway opposing him. The sounds came from down a short hall. It was a woman's voice.

He came around the door frame slowly. Lorna Luna lay naked on a bed, spread-eagled, and tied to the head and footboard. Mark cleared the room visually and charged the bathroom door. Nothing. He tried the two walk-in closets, but no one was in either. The room was safe. He turned to Lorna and untied her hands. Bruises showed on her breasts, and a large red welt darkened on her stomach. She had been crying. He untied her ankles and gave her a dressing robe from the floor.

"Who did this, Lorna?"

"Some men, two men. I hope they're gone. No, there were three of them here."

"I saw only two." Mark ran to the door and began a quiet search of the rest of the house, starting on the second floor. He found no one there so worked down to the first floor. In one room he found the maid who had let him in the front door. She was tied to a chair and gagged. Her dress had been ripped, revealing one breast. The girl was sobbing.

Mark untied her, took off the gag, and calmed her so she would talk.

119

"He grabbed me and tied me up and ripped open my dress."

"Is he still here? Where did he go?"

"When he saw the dead man in the hall, he got frightened and ran out the front door. I heard him go down the steps. He said he was getting as far away from here as he could."

Mark took the girl back upstairs with him and found Lorna still sitting on the edge of the bed. From her expression he couldn't tell what she was thinking.

"Lorna, are you all right?"

She made no reply.

"Lorna, should I call your doctor?"

At that she stirred, shook her head. "No, no. I'm all right. I was just trying to think how to say thank you. I haven't got a script for this. I don't know what words to use."

"You did fine. Now tell me what happened. Why didn't you keep the security as I suggested?"

"I don't know. I had them here for a day, and then it seemed so silly. So I told them to go home. Then today a man came and said he wanted to see you. He pushed his way into the house, and two more men came in. They said they wanted me to call the tall, dark guy who was here before. Somehow they knew that I had your phone number. They hit me and did all sorts of things to me until I told them I would call. They made me leave a message. I'm sorry."

"Why did they want me to come here?"

"I thought you knew. So they could kill you. They talked about it all the time they waited. Then I heard the shooting, so I thought . . ."

"They missed."

"I'm glad, you marvelous boy."

120

"Promise me that you'll put the security back on to-morrow."

"I will; I will."

"Now, is there anything else I can do?"

"Janette tells me there's an honest-to-God dead man in my hallway downstairs."

"Yes, there seems to be," Mark admitted.

"Aren't you going to call the police?"

"No, I don't want to get involved in that. One of his friends shot him in the neck when he was trying to shoot me. Too bad for him. But I'm sure you can tell all that to the police just as well as I can. I suggest you phone them now before a neighbor does."

"Yes, that's a good idea."

"I better be going. If you have any more problems, I won't be able to help you. You're on your own now."

"Not even your phone number?" Lorna said.

"The number's disconnected."

"Then I'll have to wait for you to call me."

Mark smiled, walked out of the bedroom, down the steps, and ran out the front door to the street. He got in his car and drove away from the place, glad that no neighbors had notified the touchy Beverly Hills police about the shots.

In the front window of the second floor of Lorna's big house, Janette watched through the dimness of the street lights as Mark ran down the steps to the street and to his car. She smiled as Mark got in his car, made a U-turn, and drove away. Then Janette ran back to Lorna's room.

"He's gone," she told Lorna.

The star dropped her robe and walked naked toward the young girl. She kissed her hard on the lips, squealed in delight, and jumped on the king-sized bed.

"Hurry, darling, tie me up again. Tie me tight, and

121

then we can get back to what we started before that awful man burst in here," Lorna said.

"But what about the dead one downstairs?" Janette asked, quickly unzipping her maid's dress and stepping out of it.

"Oh, pooh, he's dead. An hour more or less won't matter any to him. Then we'll both have a shower, and we'll call my old friend, the chief of police. You'll have to help me with some good lines to say when he comes. All we have to do is tell him to go out and find Lance Lansing. Actors are never hard to locate, and I still think Lance is an actor of some kind."

Lorna Luna grimaced as Janette tied her hand to the top of the bed with a scarf.

Chapter 13

HELLO, CENTRAL CASTING?

It was nearly two o'clock in the morning when Mark made the U-turn near Lorna Luna's house and drove back toward Hollywood. He evaluated the mission so far and felt as if he were in a sea of quicksand. He kept finding bits and pieces of flotsam to cling to, but they quickly sank out of sight when he tried to assemble them, and he was back floundering again.

Lorna, for instance. How did he know when she was acting and when she wasn't? She was the perfect actress on stage. The audience believed every line, every gesture; she became the character. But how did he peel that acting away and find the real Lorna Luna? And more important, how did he know if she were reading a script to him or simply out-and-out lying? Something about her whole story tonight didn't jibe. It had been too obvious a setup, a trap. A rather crude attempt to blow his head off. Mark drove along nighttime Santa Monica Boulevard. This was the time the street took on a whole new character, with the night people out, more black-and-white patrol cars than he saw during the day, and some wildly strange people on the sidewalks.

He kept remembering Lorna. There was one part of

her scene that couldn't have been faked. She was tied, spread-eagled to the bed, and she did have large bruises on her breasts and another one on her flat belly. She certainly had seemed to be in shock and despair when he found her. But how many women had he seen just after they had been raped or beaten? One, maybe two. He had no yardstick for measurement.

But the bruises—those could not be faked. He shook his head in frustration. He had to quit second-guessing situations and work with the facts.

What else did he have? His mind clicked back over the mission until he came to the four phone numbers he had found in Johnathan Westerly's office. Four numbers. One had been that of GTA's switchboard. What about the other three? He had given them to Angie just this evening. She couldn't have done anything on them yet.

He should try the old policeman's trick. It wouldn't hurt to give it a go. Mark pulled over at an unlit telephone booth and pushed a dime in the slot. At least the L.A. phone calls still cost only a dime. He dialed the operator, and when she came on, he went into his act.

"This is Detective Wilson. I have an emergency. Would you connect me with your supervisor?"

"Yes, sir."

"This is Miss Martin. Can I help you?"

"This is Detective Wilson with Narcotics. I'm on an investigation, telephoning a contact, a snitch. She was giving me some vital information on one of my cases. Halfway through she began gasping and choking and calling for help. Then she dropped the phone, and I couldn't raise anyone else there. She never tells me where she's calling from."

"What kind of help do you need?"

124

"According to department regulations, you're empowered to give me the address of that phone number. I need it quickly so I can try and save that girl's life."

"I'll need your badge number, station, and what the emergency is, Detective Wilson."

"Right. I'm Badge 218, central. The emergency is so I can send an ambulance to that address and have dispatch radio the closest patrol car in the area to investigate."

"Just a moment while I check my unit manager."

There were twenty seconds of dead air, and the supervisor was back on the phone.

"I'll need your first name and initial, please."

"John F. Can you hurry, please?"

"We show no central precinct."

"For God's sakes, that's central division. How long have you been around here?"

"Just one moment." There was a pause. "Sir, that number is listed as being installed at 13067 Vine Street."

"At 13067 Vine. Thanks." Mark hung up, smiling. It usually worked. He had the number memorized as he ran back to his rented LTD and drove to Vine Street.

Vine—Hollywood and Vine—the traditional heart of Hollywood, now the hangout for all sorts of weird creatures parading around as humans. He had no idea where 13067 was.

Mark found it fifteen minutes later. It was a three-story block building with its own ground floor entrance and the number over the door in large letters. It was Dunnco Distributing. Mark parked in front and looked at the windows. All he could see were venetian blinds and white-painted stucco. Dunnco Distributing could be a wholesaler for anything. How did that tie in with

GTA where he had found the number? Mark got back to the main stem and drove to his motel.

The Penetrator fell on his bed at three o'clock and was awakened promptly at seven-thirty that morning by a small message from his mental alarm. Mark sat up in bed and yawned. Why didn't he just lie back down and go to sleep until noon? Great idea!

With that out of the way, he got up, showered, shaved and called Angelina Perez. She answered quickly.

"Is this the Perez Information Service?" Mark asked.

"Young man. If you're ever going to succeed with this obscene phone call business, you're going to have to learn how to disguise your voice. Are you awake, Mark, or just up?"

"Neither. Did you get any ID on those numbers yet? I'd guess you haven't since nothing is open."

"I got the addresses last night from a friend of mine who works for the LAPD. At least he got me two out of the three. One is a disconnect, one is Dunnco Distributing, and the other is Investments Unlimited."

"So that's not much help."

"It could be."

"Why, oh, fount of knowledge, do you lead me on that way?"

Angie laughed. "Well, I admit it isn't much, but Dunnco Distributing is the firm that circulates the Jeffrey Scott Duncann Production films. National distributors. And we found out yesterday that Lorna Luna had made a dozen feature films for Duncann."

"You're grasping at straws, Angie. Nothing so far ties in with GTA at all. That's the tie in we need." He tried to think it through. The line was silent.

"Hey, you still there?" she asked.

126

"Yes."

"Good. Did you hear the morning news? Your friend Lorna Luna found a dead man in her house last night. She doesn't know a thing about it. Said her secretary drove her home from a movie, and they found her front door open and the body inside. Police said he had been shot in the neck and bled to death. They found evidence of a gunfight inside the house, but neighbors reported hearing nothing unusual."

"Interesting," Mark said. "Have you had breakfast?"

"No."

"I'll pick you up in half an hour if you're hungry. I have some work you can help me with."

"I'll be ready."

Over the number two breakfast at John-Boy's Restaurant, they talked it out.

"Every corporation has to file papers with the state showing their corporate ownership, directors, and officers. It's a long shot, but why don't we go to the state office building and see what we can find on these three firms."

"Easy. I have an excop buddy who works for the state. He should be able to help us." She furrowed her forehead with three wrinkles and pointed her fork. "Hey, don't you want those hash browns?"

Mark grinned and scooped them up and put them on her plate.

"Where do you put all that food?"

"I'm a hard feeder. I had to put on seven pounds to get into the LAPD when I joined. I didn't think I was ever going to make it. For my last physical I drank four glasses of water just before the weigh-in."

"And you made it." Mark smiled at her. "You must have been the prettiest cop on the force."

She smiled and tilted her head a little to one side.

127

"Why thank you very much. I appreciate that. I wasn't, of course, but it's nice to hear you say it."

"What did they have you doing?"

"On a beat, a two-cop car. We were in a better class neighborhood where we seldom had a call. I never drew my service revolver in my whole year on the beat except for target practice."

"Be glad, lady. Be glad of that."

She finished the hash browns and the rest of the third egg and coffee. "I got to thinking last night—here I am working with you, shooting people to help you, and I don't even know your last name."

Mark sighed. "Yes, you're right. And now I wish you didn't even know my first name. Wish Joey hadn't told you. But we can't change that."

She started to say something, but he held up his hand to stop her.

"Let me tell you a short little story. I was working a tough case with some real bad dudes in Detroit. They were trying to stop me anyway they could. I had talked to a young girl one night because she was a friend of a friend, and I gave her a ride home after some trouble. She'd never seen me before that night, didn't know my name, what I did, where I was from, not even where I was staying.

"Somehow they found out about her, kidnapped her, questioned her, tortured her, then got word to me that she was hurt and needed help. They offered a trade. but I knew those scum; I knew how they worked. I agreed to the trade, my information for the girl. But I knew she was already dead. That's the way they played the game. It was all their rules. We found her the next day."

He sipped at his coffee.

"Then I made a vow, Angie, never to get close to

128

another human being. Never to give anyone a handle on me, never to allow anyone leverage against me. And I was determined that not one innocent person would die simply because they had brushed against my life, no matter how briefly. That's why I wish you weren't sitting there talking to me. And that's also the reason I'm glad that you are."

She reached out and touched his hand. "I'm sorry, Mark. I should have understood. You're not just another private investigator. I knew that from the start. You must be with the Company."

Mark shook his head. "I'm not the Company type. Now, I think it's time we forget all this and get down to the state office building. The only reason we're going together is that these people we're working against are not as bloodthirsty as most I've seen. I think the worst of them here have already been eliminated."

Angie watched him from deep brown and concerned eyes as they drove to the downtown section of Los Angeles. "Mark, no more questions from me. I understand something of the situation you're in without knowing all about it. I've been in a few tough spots myself. I'll help you in any way that I can."

"Thanks, Perez. If you could find me a place to park, it would be a great help."

Angie smiled, knowing she had said the right thing. For the first time she realized how lonely he must be, how much of a one-man force he had to be. She didn't know who he worked for or why, or exactly what he did, but she was satisfied. She also understood his need to make a flip comment now so not too much of his feelings would show through.

Inside the building it went more smoothly than Mark had thought it would. Angie telephoned someone from the lobby, and they went up to the sixth floor and

129

along the hall to 611. A tall, well-dressed Mexican-American man let out a whoop of glee when he saw Angie come in the door. He ran past three desks to her and swept her up in his arms and kissed her on the cheek. "It's good to see you. It's been too long."

She enjoyed the double spin as he whirled her around and kissed her cheek again before he put her down. It didn't embarrass her in the slightest. She turned and caught Mark's hand.

"Pete, this is a friend of mine. His name is Friend. Friend, say hello to Pete Valesquez. Everyone calls him Val."

Val took Mark's hand firmly, his eyes meeting Mark's evenly, with a touch of curiosity.

"Friend, good to meet you. Any friend of Angie's . . ." He let it hang. His voice lowered. "Angie, you back with the Company?"

"No, I'm not. You still have that office? I need some minor-type help."

"Help? Girl, I helped you for a solid six months in that beat-up prowl car. How can I stop now?"

"Sure, you helped me, right up until we had that baby to deliver in the back seat of the black-and-white. Then suddenly you needed to use the radio to call the hospital."

"Somebody had to." They both laughed.

Down the row of desks were two offices. They went into one, and Angie told him what they needed.

"I could have done that by phone, but I'm glad you stopped by." He lifted his brows. "Oh, this is unofficial, I take it?"

Angie nodded.

He picked up the phone and punched up the computer operator in Sacramento. It took two minutes to get into the computer; then the operator fed in the names, and five seconds later Val began writing down names and addresses. There were six names on Investments Unlimited, all owners, directors. GTA had three names, all officers. Dunnco Distributing had only four names, all seemingly members of Duncann's immediate family.

"I hope you can read my writing," Val said. He pushed the yellow pad toward Angie. It was written in the block printing letters and figures that are a must on police reports for all nontyping officers. Angie tore off the page and handed it to Mark without reading it.

"Still glad you aren't wearing a blue suit and a badge?" she asked.

"Yes. I left a year after you did. That second slug that hit me did the trick. It was high, just nicked a lung, and put me between the sheets for two months. That did it. I started looking for another job as soon as I could use a telephone." Val reached over and lifted Angie's brown purse. He laughed. "You still pack that cannon?"

She nodded.

"Why you like that big old .45 is beyond me."

They talked about their days on the force for ten minutes more before Angie stood up.

"Val, it's been great talking to you again. Say hello for me to Alicia and the *ninos*."

A few minutes later they were alone in the elevator, and Angie and Mark both looked at the yellow paper. There were no duplicate names on any of the three lists. But there were two identical addresses: 21212 Alta Vista in Beverly Hills.

Mark smiled, and Angie let out a whoop of delight.

"At least we have one small matchup," Angie said. "One of the addresses is for an officer on GTA and one for the corporate secretary for Investments Unlimited. At least it's the beginning of a tie."

"But it's not much more than we knew before," Mark said.

In the car they compared the lists again but found no other duplications.

"Let's pay a call on 21212 Alta Vista and see who is home," Mark said.

It was almost noon by the time they crawled through the Friday rush-hour traffic and got into Beverly Hills. They cruised Alta Vista and came up empty.

"No 21212 Alta Vista," Angie said. "There's a 21218 and a 21210, but the houses are side by side. No room for another house in there anyplace."

"The old phony address trick."

"Which means something else is probably crooked as well."

"Right. How would you like to play my secretary for a while?" Mark asked.

"Sounds like we're going to impersonate a state official."

"Not until we find a quiet, empty phone booth."

Five minutes later they located a phone booth away from the busy streets. Angie made a call to GTA.

"Yes, hello, Global Talent Agency? This is Mr. Dickerman's secretary at the California Corporation Office in Sacramento. He's calling for your GTA corporate secretary, listed here as a Mr. Ambrose Dunsmuir. Is he in?"

"Just a moment. I'll ring the office."

A new voice came on the phone.

"Mr. Dunsmuir's office."

"Is he in? Mr. Dickerman of the California Corporations Office in Sacramento is calling."

"Just a moment."

The voice that came next was male and smoothly casual.

"Ambrose Dunsmuir here."

"Just a moment for Mr. Dickerman," Angie grinned and passed the phone to Mark.

"Dunsmuir? Dickerman here, State Corporations office in Sacramento. Say, we've got some problems with GTA. A spot check of our records on your corporate papers shows that we've been getting mail returned, marked no such number on an address in Beverly Hills. Could you give me some answers?"

"Oh, a wrong address? Doesn't seem likely. What's the name and address? There must be some simple explanation."

"The name listed is yours, and the address is 21212 Alta Vista, Beverly Hills. Our field man reports there's no such number on that street. If you can't give me some reasonable explanation, I'll have to calendar your corporation for a disciplinary hearing in my office no later than next week for all of your corporate officers."

"Mr. Dickerman, I assure you there's only a minor mistake here. I understand the problem now. That Alta Vista address is in Santa Barbara where my exwife lives. The secretary here simply put down the wrong address combination on the corporate papers for me. I don't know how a thing like that could have slipped through our final check."

"That does sound possible. What is your official address now, Mr. Dunsmuir?"

"What? Oh, I'm at 814 Beverly Lane in Beverly Hills."

"Fine. That should straighten it out. You realize it's a felony to misrepresent either names or addresses on a corporate affadavit? Please send a notarized correction copy of that page of your corporate papers to this office within forty-eight hours, and you should avoid any prosecution."

"Yes, sir, Mr. Dickerman. I'll be sure to take care of that immediately."

Mark hung up, and Angie let out a little chortle of glee.

"Did he say 814 Beverly Lane?"

"That's what you just heard through the old ear piece."

"Now we have a real tie. That is exactly the address given by Jeffrey Scott Duncann on his Dunnco Distributing corporate papers. Duncann must own both GTA and Investments Unlimited!"

Chapter 14

SPECIAL EFFECTS SET ... AND ROLLING!

Angie and Mark stood there in the Beverly Hills phone booth grinning at each other.

"By Jove, I think we've got it!" Angie said in a thick Cockney accent.

Mark laughed. "Knowing it is easy. When you have to prove it in court is the hard part."

"Aye, there's the rub!"

Mark caught her hand and pulled her out of the phone booth and toward the car.

"I think you're having an English attack."

Back in the car Angie dropped her accent. "There's more you should know about our friend, Jeffrey Scott Duncann. He's not the gentle, lily-white, benevolent producer you may have heard about."

She quickly filled in Mark with the background on Duncann over the past two years, including his troubles with the forged checks, the subsequent blacklisting of his production company, and the smashing success of his space epic.

"So there Duncann sat, a man with a brilliant record as a director and producer, and he couldn't hire a professional crew to shoot a movie. He must have been outrageously bitter and furious."

"So he buys up all the talent in Hollywood," Mark said. "He tries to corner the market on actors and actresses so he can dictate terms to the other studios."

"Right. With his clout now, he can put any producer he picks out of business. He simply does not let any of his stars sign to work for that outfit." She looked at Mark. "What's our next step?"

"I think we should see this man in person."

"That shouldn't be too hard. Tonight is the much anticipated Screen Arts Ball. It's the best ticket in town, and everyone has been looking forward to it for weeks. GTA is throwing the big bash and they've invited half the town. All of their stars and talent will be there, all the top producers, independents, directors, cameramen, sound men . . . probably half the industry. It's being held in the old mansion once owned by Marsha Marlowe, the silent screen star. It just happens that Joey gave me his pair of tickets about two weeks ago. Interested?"

"Will Duncann be there?"

She thought a moment. "I'd guess he will be. He owns GTA; this is his baby. He probably planned the whole thing. This might be the time to come out of the closet and let Hollywood know just how much power he has over them. Yes, knowing a little about Duncann, that's what I think he'll do."

"Then I wouldn't miss it."

"Oh, one thing I forgot to tell you. This is a costume ball. You must have a costume on, or you can't get in the gate."

"One of those."

"Right. Not quite the Beaux Arts Ball but almost. Lots of wild costumes and animals and probably a few slave girls with nothing on but their imagination."

136

"I'm going to enjoy this party. Tell me when to pick you up."

That evening at eight o'clock, Mark and Angie parked four blocks from the Marlow mansion and walked up to the gate. The guard was pulling at a champagne bottle and waved them through without looking at their passes.

Angie came as a harem girl, with see-through flimsy pants, a jeweled bikini top, and her black hair covered with a froth of silk scarves. A small black mask covered her eyes.

Mark looked like Zorro with a black, wide-brimmed hat, cape, black mask, and a long wide saber at his side in a black sheath.

The mansion had been set up for a horror film a month before, and after shooting, the special effects had been left in place or rebuilt and activated. Additional surprises had been put in, and the invitation claimed there were more shockers than anyone had seen before—but everything would be ultimately safe. However, no guarantees were given for the easily frightened against the possibility of a fright heart attack. The film people loved the spoof and the make-believe.

Black-lighted arrows pointed the way through the lavish grounds. There was no route directly into the house. First, the guests had to run the gauntlet. At the first turn a granite wall almost fell on the guests but stopped before crushing anyone with its polyfoam granite blocks. The wall stopped just in time, machinery ground, and the wall teetered back into place to await the next unsuspecting partygoer to trip the automatic switch planted in the footpath.

When the wall toppled, Angie jumped back and grabbed Mark, then saw what it was and laughed.

They had agreed that they could stay together since no one could readily identify either of them in their masks.

The next arrow showed the way around a corner where a full-grown tiger roared at them and lunged forward to the end of a three-eighths-inch thick, steel link chain. Mark hoped the chain held all night and that the cat didn't get overly excited.

Suddenly a ghostly form floated at them from the darkness and came closer. It was an apparition, an evil-looking wispy creature with its head in its hand, moving towards them. They ducked as the bloody sight passed directly over them. Mark reached up and tried to touch it. His hand went right through the image.

"A holograph," Mark said.

She held his hand tighter. "I know it's all make-believe, but that thing scares me silly," Angie said.

"The special effects men will be pleased," Mark told her. They wound through a small rose garden with dozens of blooms all spotlighted and came to a tennis court. The court was slippery, and they realized it was covered with a sheet of ice. They slid, slipped, and at last fell down before they made it to the other side.

"Ice? That's crazy." Angie said. "Who expects ice outside in Beverly Hills in the middle of summer, or in winter for that matter?"

On the other side of the ice the black-lighted arrows pointed through the doors of an Old West saloon. Mark pushed the bat doors open, and they heard a chorus of shots from inside. Instinctively Mark jumped back and reached for the .45 in his belt. But before he drew it, a boisterous cowboy jolted through the swinging doors with a second man right behind him. They fought a knock-down stunt man scenario until neither man could get up. At that time a third cowboy came swaggering from the saloon doors and shot the other two with his six gun. A moment later all three jumped up and vanished into the darkness.

Inside the saloon false front were the first trays of drinks.

"Champagne, right this way," a young man said and gave them each a long-stemmed plastic glass filled with bubbly, and moved to the next group.

"Now this is class," Mark said. "I wonder where the big brass of GTA is, and how I'll be able to find this J.S. Duncann?"

"Stick with me, kid. I'll point him out," Angie said.

Just outside the saloon champagne bar, a giant spider fell within inches of them, gave off some hissing and spurts of white smoke, and retreated to wait for the next victim.

"This could be fun if it wasn't work," Mark said. He caught Angie's hand and led her toward the next arrow, which showed the way into a covered grape arbor. Halfway through they heard voices, low at first, then louder. They stopped.

"Darling, you just go right ahead and feel me there all you want to. Nobody can see us, and I like it. Fantastic! I want you to put your hand right inside."

A man's voice responded. "But what about your husband?"

"Oh, he's probably into his third glass of champagne already and trying to get his hands on one of those slave girls."

"I shouldn't."

"Please, I want you to!"

Further down the arbor path Mark used his night sight to spot the three-foot-square pressure pad in the walk that triggered the next recorded voices.

"Oh, yes, yes, darling!" the woman said.

139

"Oh, but you're beautiful. Does the grass hurt your back? Move just a little, yes, there."

"Ohhhhhhhh, marvelous, sweetheart, that's so good, so hard and good!"

Then came two sharp reports, sound of shots, and the woman screamed, then moaned. Another shot and the man cried out.

"How . . . how did you know?" the man asked.

Another man's voice came on. "How do you think? She told me where you'd be." The man laughed again, and there was the sound of another shot.

Angie giggled. "We get a running soap opera as we go along."

"Soap opera?" Mark said, straight-faced. "I thought they were real people back there."

When they came out of the arbor, the arrows of black light pointed them toward the pool. Two men fought with sabers around the edge of the water. When six or eight people had gathered to watch, one dueler screamed, grasped his chest, and fell into the wetness.

"How much more of this is there?" Mark asked.

"It's five acres of lawns, gardens, and swimming pools, so I'd guess there's quite a lot more."

"Then let's go this way," Mark said. They walked around the pool in the opposite direction that the arrows pointed, found three more sets of swordsmen practicing behind some trees and one man changing his wet clothes to dry ones.

Mark had seen French doors opening on a patio. They edged into the patio and walked through the French doors as if they were coming back inside. It worked.

They were near one of the large ballrooms in the mansion. This one had been decorated with blue and white, the GTA colors. Everywhere were men and women in wild clothes. Some of the getups were elaborate rented costumes, some so natural there was almost no costume showing except skin. One couple was joined at the waist as Siamese twins.

The champagne was pink in this room. Mark and Angie picked glasses off a moving tray and mingled.

"None of the brass are here that I can see," Angie said. They wandered from one beautiful room to another. It was a palace with marble steps, ornate fixtures, brilliant oil paintings in oversized frames, and delicate stained-glass windows. Mark had never seen so many marble sculptures in his life.

"A fantastic house," Angie said pulling at his Zorro cape.

"But I'd hate to pay the rent or the taxes," Mark said.

There was little form or structure to the party. About an hour later they had the grand procession with the judging of all contestants' costumes. Half the guests participated. A nude male with his hair up in curlers won the men's division for best male costume, and a six-foot-four-inch girl dressed entirely in pink ostrich feathers won for the best female costume.

Displays here and there extolled the virtues of GTA, what a perfect agency to work for. Some showed the GTA clients in the biggest movies of the year.

By eleven-thirty the free champagne was taking its toll. Mark also saw dozens of guests snorting cocaine and popping pills, and there was the general sweet, smokey smell of marijuana in almost every room.

Mark and Angie circled back to the hot hors d'oeuvres table and nibbled for a moment. Then Angie tugged at Mark's cape.

"He's here, Mark. It's Mr. Duncann himself. Over there. He's the paunchy one, the look alike for Alfred

141

Hitchcock, with balding head and all. He's just coming in the door."

Mark spotted the man, made sure he had the right one.

"You stay here," Mark said. He walked toward the producer, working quickly across the crowded room. Mark waited until the man was through talking with someone, and then the Penetrator put a commanding hand on his shoulder.

"Mr. Duncann, I have to talk to you. I know that you own Global Talent Agency, and that makes you an accessory to murder at least twice. The game is over, Duncann. I can prove you own GTA and that you have it for reasons of pure vengeance. What I'm telling you is you're caught, and the homicide people are on their way here right now to arrest you for murder one."

Duncann stared at Mark for a moment, and when he was sure the man was not drunk or joking, he laughed nervously. "I don't know what you're talking about, sir. I own nothing but my production company. All the big producers are here tonight."

"I can prove you own GTA, Duncann. And that means you're guilty of murder, mayhem, assault and battery, coercion, conspiracy—enough to put you away for fifty years at least."

Duncann tried to leave, but Mark's grip tightened on his shoulder. He turned back and stared at Mark. Slowly something seemed to register on the older man's face, and he nodded.

"All right, out onto the back veranda. I'll show you how you are wrong."

This time when he tried to turn, Mark let him go but was right behind him. Soon they stood alone on a wooden-floored balcony, a half story off the ground, on the south side of the house.

"Now, young man, I don't know what on earth you're talking about. I'm busy working on my sequel to *Starbound Space War*. Surely you've heard of my smashingly successful picture."

"You're not working on anything, Duncann. You can't even hire a second-rate cameraman. You're banned, blacklisted. You'll never make another feature in this town, and you know it. You're all washed up, a has-been. And on top of that your GTA goons have been killing people. That makes you responsible, and you'll be in the gas chamber right alongside them."

"Don't say that!" Duncann roared. He stomped his foot in anger, then smiled as a trap door opened and dropped him out of sight. The wooden panel closed at once, and Mark couldn't find the trigger.

He checked both sides of the twenty-foot-wide screened porch. Then he saw the producer emerging from a small gazebo fifty feet into the garden. Mark decided he could make faster time overland than through the underground passage. He found a door, vaulted down the steps, and ran into a maze-like garden after Duncann. Only part of the maze was floodlighted here. But Mark soon discovered this was another part of the gauntlet the guests had to run before getting inside the house to the party.

The Penetrator ran up and down the privet hedges searching for Duncann. Thick rows of roses came next, and Mark saw Duncann panting along ahead of him, almost out of the maze.

The rows of roses were too tall to jump over and set too thickly to wiggle through but low enough to see over, which increased Mark's frustration. He saw Duncann break out of the maze, panting and gasping for breath, and head in the side door of the west wing of the mansion.

Mark tried to break through the end of a privet hedge, only to find a wire fence in the center. At last he located the post holding up the wire and used that to vault over the privet, losing his cape and snagging his saber sheath on the thicket. He pulled the sheath loose and fell on his shoulder but rolled forward to ease the blow and landed on his feet, running.

Mark went through the same door Duncann had, but the fat man was nowhere around. The Penetrator began another search. About half the guests now had taken off their masks, but Mark left his on. He heard a commotion in the main ballroom, which was over a hundred feet long and half that wide. By the time Mark got there, Duncann had gathered around him twenty of his biggest and most famous stars on a platform in the center of the room. There were about three hundred people crowded into the rest of the ballroom. They quieted as Duncann took a microphone.

"Friends, guests, everyone. Welcome to this little party. We hope you like it. You may remember me, although most of you haven't been speaking to me lately. I'm the guy you treat like poison, remember? I run the production company none of you will work for, afraid you'll dirty your dainty white reputations. Well, my fair-weather friends, I have news for you. You have been working with me for the past year. You just didn't know it. Every time you used an actor or a star from Global Talent Agency, you were working with Jeffrey Scott Duncann, because I own GTA lock, stock, and thespian."

An excited stuttering of talk swept back and forth through the room of movie people.

"None of you have really thought what that means

144

yet, have you? I now control ninety percent of the best talent in the English-speaking world. Not bad for one year, not bad at all."

Mark worked his way to the front of the audience. He stood with his hands on his hips, then drew the saber, and walked toward Duncann. The producer saw Mark and moved back slightly. The stars smiled, knowing it was more of the make-believe they had witnessed all night.

"Not one step farther, sir!" Duncann bellowed in his best melodramatic voice. "I don't know who you are, but I won't have any violence here."

Mark took another step. Duncann held out a small black box the size of a cigarette package and pushed on it. There was a grinding and creaking, and everyone looked up. From over the small platform in the center of the room, a ring of steel bars came down from the ceiling. The ring was fifteen feet across and circled the platform that had been built there. Before anyone thought to move, the half-inch thick steel bars had lowered to the floor. They extended from the floor to the twenty-foot ceiling and now trapped the twenty stars inside along with Duncann.

"A little surprise for you, folks; it's from a competitive movie we won't mention."

Mark saw the danger at once. Duncann had some other tricks, he was sure. The Penetrator knew the guests thought he was part of this little play. So he acted the part, knowing Duncann would react in panic and perhaps show his hand.

Using his best melodramatic voice, Mark responded quickly to Duncann by sheathing his saber and pulling out his .45 automatic.

"My God, sir! I can't let you trap the fair maidens. I'll have it out with you now!"

The crowd cheered Mark. His presence and his obvious gun that would not be stopped by the steel bars brought beads of perspiration to the producer's bald head. His eyes widened in surprise. Duncann pushed another button on his black box, and a section of the floor opened in front of him. A small platform rose from the floor, and on it all could see a large melodramatic-looking bomb. It was a foot square, made up of what looked like two dozen sticks of dynamite, surrounded by a packed ring of quarter-pound bars of plastic explosive. Mark knew exactly what it was, plastique, C-3, from the color-coding on the outer wrapping.

Mark tensed. Duncann smiled.

"A bomb, ladies and gentlemen. If I had a handlebar moustache, I would surely twirl it. You really don't understand yet, do you? Oh, yes, this is a real bomb." He took another small box from his pocket and pulled out a foot-long antenna. "And so is this real. It's the radio trigger to detonate the bomb. This small bit of explosive is enough to level this mansion and half the buildings within a block of here. It would blow out the windows in every Beverly Hills mansion for half a mile. Incidentally, it would blow all of us into kingdom come in the flash of an eyelash. Now do some of you understand?"

The crowd began edging backward. More moved out of the doors and began running for the exits. Duncann laughed. He watched them go for a moment, then stomped on the floor, and another section of the floor swung upward, revealing a stairway. Seconds later Duncann was gone, and the trapdoor had closed tightly. Brad Russell ran from the cowering group of stars and began stomping on the floor where Duncann had stood, but nothing happened. He turned to the crowd.

"Don't just stand there, idiots, the party's over. Call the police, for God's sakes. That's a real bomb. I've seen enough of them before. J.S. Duncann has flipped his wig! That bomb could go off at any time."

Chapter 15

"OKAY, PEOPLE, THAT'S A WRAP!"

Before anyone else could move, two large screens lit up, one on each end of the long ballroom. They were closed circuit television screens ten feet square. The houselights in the room came down on a slow rheostat, and everyone turned to watch J.S. Duncann himself sputtering into the camera.

"Now listen to me, every Tom, Dick, and Jane of you. I helped build this town, helped start this whole industry that you work in. You can't just throw me out like an old shoe. I've misplaced more know-how about making movies than most of you will ever learn.

"Nobody can push around J.S. Duncann. I won't allow it. And now I have the whole damn industry right where I want you. Twentieth Century, you do what I say, or you get no more talent for your hogwash. Universal, you think you're so hot with all your TV series and TV movies going. I've got news for you, Universal. I have all but two of your series stars signed to contracts, and none of them will work if I tell them not to. I can wipe out your TV series in a month by telling my clients not to come to work. I can squeeze you out and make you go broke in six months, waltz in, and take over what's left.

"Do you hear me out there? I've got the clout, the power, the money, and the know-how. I've got it all now. Nobody can stop me. There is no way.

"Why did all this happen? Simply because I borrowed a few thousand dollars from my own company through the use of a couple of names of friends of mine. I've made millions for all those people, and now they rail against some little thing like this. Dammit! I paid back all the money, the District Atorney never laid a glove on me, no prosecution at all. So why all the hate shit I get from Hollywood? Jealousy.

"Think you're so damn pure out there? Hell, I know a dozen producers who did things a thousand times worse than I did. Only I got caught. So think about that when you're standing there alone and angry in the unemployment line. Think about that when you come to GTA to try to get on our list. And you producers think about that as you sit in your overpriced offices with a production crew standing by at twenty thousand dollars an hour when you don't have a star in front of your cameras."

Mark eased out of the room. He had to find Duncann and stop all this. He had taken a closer look at the bomb and saw that it was genuine. At least everything looked right, so it could be the real thing. He couldn't take any chances with this many people around. There was no way to defuse the bomb or disarm it as long as Duncann held the trigger. It could be a break-to-make latch-up. So the bomb was his first mission.

Mark stood at the door for a moment, looking at the best actors in the world cooped up like chickens. Hostages! The word beat through his brain. What else had Duncann planned? He had to find the man fast. Upstairs or down? He knew Duncann had moved downward in his escape, but they were on the second floor here, and Mark guessed that the producer was upstairs. Mark took the ornate open staircase steps three at a time, the sword banging him on the side at every step. He didn't want to take the time to remove it.

Upstairs he found a series of bedrooms, some occupied by oblivious thrashing bodies. One room was a library. Mark paused and went inside. The books looked unusually straight and orderly. It was obvious that they were painted on. He pushed one, but it wouldn't move. He pulled and tried to slide them. That was the key. A whole section of the book panel moved smoothly to one side, revealing three TV monitors. There were twelve of them stacked on the bookshelves, twelve monitors for twelve cameras. Mark guessed that each of the bedrooms had a camera hidden in a lighting fixture.

Tape? Could Duncann's tirade be on a video tape recording? Why not? He didn't say anything he wouldn't have known before tonight's party. Mark looked around the library and found more hidden panels. Behind one was a door that opened into a master control room. A casette TV recorder spun around, evidently feeding signals into the closed-circuit TV screens downstairs. Small TV cameras, lights, and a ministudio made up the rest of the room. Everything was in good working order.

But J.S. Duncann was not there.

Mark tried to figure where he might be. What would his ego demand? He would want to be somewhere to watch and observe the reaction of his audience. But where? There were no balconies in the big ballroom. Somewhere on the large grounds? No.

On his way down the steps the Penetrator looked

150

out the front windows and saw three police cars pull up. Behind them came a lumbering truck pulling a "garbage" can steel bomb basket on a trailer. The Los Angeles bomb squad was helping out the locals.

· The bomb still worried the Penetrator. He couldn't get to it on the second floor, but what about from below? Yes, below! The catch didn't release the trapdoor when Brad Russell stomped on it, which meant Duncann must have locked it on his way out. Where would that exact spot be on the first floor? It was directly below the center of the ballroom.

Mark ran to the first floor and met dozens of people coming down the steps and away from the ballroom. The tirade was over, they said. The producer told everyone to leave at once. He didn't want to kill them all.

Mark found a room he thought could be the right one, but it wasn't. There was nothing on the ceiling at all. He tried two more rooms and on the third found what he wanted. It had a new stairway built right up the center of the room to the ceiling. Mark found the mechanism at once; spring-loaded hinges held the door down. A block of wood in place kept the door locked down. Mark removed the block, pulled back on a lever, and the trap door popped open. At once he heard a chorus of shouts of joy from the twenty actors in the cage.

Mark didn't have to do a thing. He heard the commanding voice of Brad Russell shouting everyone down, demanding that they form a line with the women first, and they came down the steps in a steady and even procession. Three minutes later Brad Russell came down, grinned, and shook Mark's hand.

"Been doing any running lately?" he asked, his eyes twinkling.

Mark grinned around his mask. "No, but I guess I

should. I'm also going to go see your next film. You handled those people well."

"My old marine corps training. Now let's get out of here before that maniac accidentally blows us all up to San Francisco."

They did. Mark closed and relocked the trap door and ran with Brad to the front door. There were few people left in the big house. The police had set up search lights outside and were using bullhorns calling for Duncann to come out with his hands up.

Brad ran to the side door and exited. Mark waved at him and continued his search for Duncann.

He listened for a moment, heard the police bullhorn pleading again with Duncann to come out and give himself up. He hadn't really hurt anyone yet.

To Mark's surprise a bullhorn answered. It was Duncann chewing out the police. Mark couldn't hear the words, but the tone was enough. He listened again. It was on the first floor somewhere that Duncann was holed up. Quietly Mark began investigating each room, looking for Duncann. The producer would be on the street side of the house to see what the cops were doing.

In the fifth room, Mark spotted Duncann behind the heavy window drapes. He had a bullhorn and was chiding the police.

Mark couldn't sleep dart him. He had Ava with him, but it might still give Duncann the chance to press the detonation button on the black box. Or more likely Duncann might touch it as his hands began to cramp and go into spasms.

Mark took from his pocket a new item made in his lab back in the Stronghold. It was a small, yet powerful, smoke bomb. This one was not white phosphorus; it was fireproof and carried with it absolutely no

152

chance of starting a fire. It belched out thick, white smoke and in a small room could be extremely effective. Mark had wanted to add a stench factor to the smoke but hadn't made any like that yet. The smoke bomb was half again as big as a golf ball. Mark took one of two he carried and threw it hard against the wall beside Duncann. The frangible shell broke and spewed the thick smoke into the room.

Duncann screamed something into the bullhorn and came from the room rubbing his eyes, the bullhorn dangling from a strap around his neck, but his right hand still held the black box with the antenna, his finger near the destruct button.

Mark had to let him go. He couldn't chance the man hitting the destruct button on purpose or accidentally.

To Mark's surprise Duncann came out pushing Lorna Luna in front of him. She was another hostage. They vanished down the hall, and a moment later when the smoke cleared, Mark found them in another room, Duncann still shouting insults at the police through his bullhorn.

Mark threw his last smoke bomb into the room, and Duncann shouted at Mark this time. He ran from the room with Lorna in front again as protection. But he lost his grip on her hand, and she staggered one way as he ran the other.

Mark caught Lorna before she fell. She thanked him and wiped her eyes, stumbled against him again, and before Mark knew how it happened, Lorna and he had fallen and she lay on top of him. She got tangled up with his arms and legs, and soon Mark realized she was not trying to get up—she was trying to keep them both down. She was helping Duncann escape.

The ploy gave Duncann time to discard his bullhorn and run out the side door into the backyard full of more special effects that Mark had missed earlier on his short route inside the mansion.

Mark came out the side door and saw Duncann vanishing into a hedge halfway across the fairway-sized back lawn. Mark ran down a path toward the producer. Suddenly in the darkness Mark sensed something directly in front of him. He felt himself step on a rubber compression trigger mat, and a moment later he stumbled on a large disc that was starting to spin. It was like a fun house with the twelve-foot-diameter disc of wood and metal with handholds that spun around faster and faster. Only this one had no handholds. Mark tried to flatten out and stay on the disc, moving to the center where the force would lessen, but gradually the centrifical force pushed him outward.

Quickly it speeded up much too fast, and Mark knew that Duncann was at the controls and could spin him off anytime he wanted to. It would shoot Mark off the disc like a stone out of a sling or a burr off a grinding wheel.

Soon it would be too late to prevent it. Mark picked a spot of grass and tried to time it as he would throwing a newspaper from a moving bike. He had to lead the spot just enough.

He jumped.

Mark landed in a roll on the soft grass, tumbled over a dozen times, and crashed into a tree with his feet. He sat up, dazed and dizzy. Ahead in some kind of a small red-and-white striped tent he saw lights. Mark stood and tried to move that way. It took him a dozen steps to get back his balance and stop fading to the right. Then he saw another of the black-lighted arrows and realized he was still in the land of special effects.

At least he could get rid of his damned saber. He stripped off the belt and discarded the weapon, after checking to be sure he still had Ava and his .45. He looked around the grounds and could see no one. Evidently the police and the panic had cleared everyone out of the house and grounds as well. The bomb squad was probably upstairs working on the bomb. If they made one wrong move, or if Duncann pushed his finger a fraction of an inch on that button . . .

Mark stared at the lighted tent again and saw someone moving around in it. That would be Duncann. Mark ran that direction, past more arrows, and just ahead heard the whine of something familiar that he couldn't quite place. Then he had it. A huge buzz saw, the three-foot diameter saws mounted on tractors, and electric motors used to cut up firewood. He had worked around one for half the summer he spent in Oregon.

The path narrowed as rough two-by-four fences channeled him into a chute made of water-soaked boards that came down quickly into a "v" shape. A dozen feet further on he felt the gush of cold water as a stream, two feet deep, suddenly slapped him on the legs and pushed him downstream. Mark slipped and slid as the flume angled downward and at last fell, splashing head first into the slippery flume. He felt the pace of the water quicken as it slanted downward more sharply. It wasn't until then that he remembered the buzz saw. No, that couldn't be.

Almost too late he looked up and saw the shiny steel blade ahead. It had been lowered from its normal position, three feet over the water, until its chisel-sharp teeth glistened a quarter-inch deep in the fast-flowing water. Mark rocketed along toward it at what seemed incredible speed, and there was nothing he could do to stop himself.

The sides of the flume changed now from rough

wood to seamless, stainless steel, and there was absolutely no place to gain a grip.

Mark had his .45 out now and looked for an operator. Someone had to control the blade depth—that had to be Duncann. But he saw no one. Mark was twenty feet from the blade and increasing his speed by the second when he saw the arm that held the spinning saw. A neat loop of power cords extended behind the arm to allow for its vertical movement. It was a chance, his only chance.

Mark fired twice at the cord, missed because of his erratic movement in the water, and fired twice more. This time the cord erupted in a shower of sparks and smoke. The whine of the motor cut off at once, and the blade began slowing. But it wouldn't be stopped in time. It was still spinning as Mark roared up to it. He held up the barrel of the .45 to hit the saw blade and at the same time pushed himself under water as far as he could go. He heard the ringing metal-to-metal crash even under the water as the big teeth of the saw tore the gun from his grasp and flung it downstream. By then he was past the saw and came up in a pool a dozen feet below. The slide, designed as a joy ride in a wooden boat that looked like a log, had been fiendishly altered by Duncann for Mark's enjoyment.

Mark worked to the side of the pool and dug his magnum derringer from his pocket. He saw Duncann peer over a log wall at the pond, then try to rig a light so he could find the body in the pond.

Mark shot twice with the derringer, saw one of the .22-caliber long-rifle slugs rip into Duncann's thigh, and watched him crumple.

Duncann let out a roar of pain, crawled inside the candy-striped tent, and vanished. Mark knew he had to chase him. He had to tie him up or cuff him for the police. The Penetrator paused for a moment, feeling too tired to move but knowing that he must. Mark climbed the small hill to where the flume had been built and saw Duncann heading toward the front gate, limping on his wounded leg.

Mark trailed him, trying to stick to the shadows around the lighted estate yard, curious why Duncann was going to the gate. Police were all around the house, and there were some along the eight-foot steel fence around the mansion grounds.

Duncann never looked back. He walked straighter now. Mark shouted at him, and he changed directions, crawled over a low rock wall, and vanished.

Mark heard the roar without realizing what it was. He ran forward just as he heard the first scream. It came torn from the soul of a man, a gut-wrenching, blood-freezing wail of fear and despair that the earth must have heard for millions of years as the frail creatures living on its crust screamed out their frustration and anger at facing death so suddenly, so overwhelmingly.

The scream echoed and came again and again from the throat. Mark charged the wall and was about to vault over it when he stopped. Ten feet below he saw all that was left of Jeffrey Scott Duncann. His head and face were untouched. But huge, sharp claws had ripped and torn the chest, stomach, and even ribs away from Duncann's body. The full-grown tiger, still on its heavy steel-link chain, growled up at Mark, flashing large, green eyes in the one floodlight that bathed the tiger's permanent den. The cat lost interest in Mark and turned back, gnawing on the bloody meal his claws had claimed from the torso of the hated man smell.

To one side, where Duncann evidently had dropped it when he fell, lay the small black box. The antenna had snapped off and lay a dozen feet away. The black box had smashed when it hit the concrete floor and broken into several pieces.

Mark stared at the remains of the man and thought about his dreams and his anger. Then the Penetrator slid back into the darkness as a young policeman ran up to the scene from the lighted side, stared at the bloody tableau for a moment, turned, and vomited.

EPILOGUE

The following afternoon, Mark Hardin sat in Angelina's kitchen looking at the newspapers. They were filled with a dozen stories about the big Hollywood party in Beverly Hills and the mauling death of famed producer J.S. Duncann, as well as the heroics of Brad Russell, the movie's top he-man who saved the world's twenty most popular movie stars from the cage.

Angie sat across from Mark. "Wow, they really dug into the GTA tieup in a rush. Some reporter did his homework on this one. The whole Duncann plot is spread out here. The reporter says that GTA will bring in new management, and the agency will begin cutting down on its number of stars until it has less than fifty percent of the name personalities. This is to try to avoid any antitrust action by the government. They say any of their contract people who wish to can move to another agency."

"Just a bunch of sweethearts down there now," Mark said. He had read most of the accounts of the party and the death. No one had any idea what had caused Duncann to bolt from the water-slide game and plunge over the side of the wall into the tiger's permanent lair. The grounds were well-known to

Duncann, who had laid out the extra special effect games himself, according to police.

"Hey, the police said the bomb was real," Angie said. "It would have gone off if Duncann had pushed that button. The experts said the bomb would have destroyed a whole city block if it had detonated. Wow, there's a lot of expensive houses in Beverly Hills."

Mark stared out the window. It had ended, not entirely the way he had hoped, but it was clean enough. The press had no hint that the Penetrator had been there. Only Duncann knew for sure, and he was dead. Brad Russell had covered for him by admitting that he had found the trigger on the trapdoor. Mark silently thanked him for that. Russell was sharper than a lot of people gave him credit for being.

Angie frowned. "You said Lorna Luna was with Duncann at the last and tried to help him get away? Hey, she must have been working with him all the time. They do go way back. She lived with him a few years back in the fifties. She must have called you out there to her place just to set you up to be killed! Oh, I wish there were something we could charge her with."

"Not a chance," Mark said. He looked at Angelina, who wore a white peasant blouse and a bright red-and-green skirt. "Angelina, what I wish is there was some way to start this over and do it so Joey would still be alive. He was just ready to put it all together. He had a star and would have done well."

She stood, picked up all the papers, and put them away in a cupboard.

"All right. As a friend of mine used to say, that's enough of that already." Tears suddenly brimmed her eyes, and she looked away.

Mark stood and put his arms around her, holding her tenderly. "Hey, easy, easy. Both of us came out of

160

this in fine shape. Not even a bruise." He turned her face to his so he could watch her. "You're not crying about what happened here, right?" —

She nodded.

He brushed away tears from her cheeks.

"Back in Arlington we had been married for over a year," Angie began. "The Company didn't like agents to marry each other, or anyone for that matter, so we kept it a secret. They thought we were just living together, which was fine." She sniffed and blew her nose. "Then one night he came home and said he'd been given a new field assignment. In Turkey. Tom was an expert in several near-Eastern languages. He never came home. They told me all the details, but that didn't help. They buried him in Turkey somewhere. The Company doesn't like to bring home dead agents . . ."

"You don't have to tell me all this."

"Oh, yes, but I do."

She talked about Tom for an hour. How they met, what he liked to wear, his specialty with the CIA. About the time he was shot four times and survived. About their plans for the future. When she was through, she was dry-eyed and almost smiling.

"I loved that man so much I almost wanted to die when he did. Eventually I talked myself out of that." Her dark brown eyes looked up at him. "I've never told anybody a word of this, not ever before."

Mark sat there waiting.

"As Tom used to say, enough of this already. I lured you up here with the promise of a gourmet Mexican dinner, and I had better start producing. Have you ever eaten *paella*?"

"Not for ten years."

"Good." She went to the kitchen and continued working on the meal.

161

Later they ate at the small kitchen table by the soft glow of candlelight. The white wine came first, then a delicious Caesar salad before the *paella*. It was the best he had ever eaten, with the saffron rice awash with tomatoes, onions, and mild chilis, heaped with lobster chunks, boned white chicken meat, shrimps and clams. Mark ate until he thought he would overflow. On the side were flour tortillas, guacamole, and a remarkable fruit salad. Mexican chocolate topped off the meal.

An hour after they began eating, Mark pushed back from the table and gave a long, satisfied sigh. "It's a good thing I don't eat with you ever day. None of my clothes would fit."

She watched him. "Mark, you don't have to worry about me. I don't know who you're hiding from or who you work for, and I really don't know enough about you to tell anyone. I wouldn't even if they asked. You might be with the Company, and you might not. I don't care. You told me how you promised yourself you'd never get close to anyone again, never get involved. I know that's partly so no one can use that person against you. I told myself the same thing two years ago. That's why I quit the Company after Tom died. I gave one man to our flag; that should be enough." She stood and went around to him, kissed his lips gently, and stepped back.

"Mark, it's time to say goodbye. I'm not going to ask you to stay tonight, because then I'd want you to stay a week and then a year, and we both know that wouldn't work. A good field agent doesn't stay in one place that long, and you're a good field man for someone."

Mark stood, a soft smile touching his face.

"Perez, I like you. Did I ever tell you that? If I ever need a partner, I'll give you a call."

They walked to the door.

"I don't move around much, Mark. I'll be right here the next time you drop into L.A. Give me a call. Lunch, maybe."

"Lunch, yes, sometime, maybe, lunch."

She ran to him and put her arms around him, kissed him hard on the lips, and stepped back. "I had to do that once before you were gone."

"Goodbye, Angie." He went out the door and down the steps. On the street below, Mark turned and waved at the top window. Angie waved back, and then he was driving the rental back to the agency at Riverside.

Mark really didn't want to go. He had a strong desire to do a U-turn and drive back. Angie was someone he would remember for a long time. A precious memory. And if he ever did need a partner, a helper in the field . . . He refused to think about that one way or the other. Time, give it some time. As the days and months passed, some of the memories would sharpen, but most would fade. He had to leave it at that.

Angie had helped him a lot in the past few days on the case. As she said, this was her town; she knew it, knew the people. Even so, he still worked alone.

That made him think of the status board back at the Stronghold. What was coming up? What was the hottest problem? He had seen a lot of wire copy lately with speculation that someone was trying to alter the normal weather patterns.

There had been some talk about it on the East Coast, and more talk by airline pilots flying the Atlantic as well as across the U.S. It might be nothing. How could anyone alter the weather? Mark thought about it as he drove. The first thing he was going to check on when he got back to the Stronghold was the weather thing. There might be something to it after all.

Mark settled down to driving, down the Hollywood Freeway to the Pomona Freeway and out to Riverside. All the way he kept seeing dark brown eyes and the curious way that Angie tilted her head when she talked.

"Goodbye, Angie Perez," Mark said out loud and pushed down the throttle, aiming for Riverside.

THE PENETRATOR'S COMBAT CATALOG

In this, and previous volumes of Mark Hardin's adventures in crime fighting, we have covered nearly all of the arms, support equipment, and vehicles used by the Penetrator. In the future, as Mark discovers and tests new equipment, additional catalog entries will appear. It is not possible for the Penetrator to become immediately aware of all innovations in the fields of firearms, holsters, electronics, support equipment, and vehicles. In the event you, the reader, are aware of something you feel Mark Hardin might be well advised to test and possibly adopt, you may contact him by writing:

Lionel Derrick
Pinnacle Books, Inc.
One Century Plaza
2029 Century Park East
Los Angeles, CA 90067

Unless you wish to remain anonymous, credit will be given in the appropriate Combat Catalog section for any suggestions you make that Mark Hardin adopts.

Some of these items are available for retail distribution, but many are one-of-a-kind developed especially for Mark Hardin. Before buying any weapon or device, it is suggested that first you check the local, state, and federal laws. Good reading . . .

Lionel Derrick

SMOKE BALL

New to the Penetrator's arsenal against
crime is the M-1 Smoke Ball. In the past
the Penetrator has used the army-type
white phosphorus smoke grenade, which
serves the purpose well in producing
smoke but also burns down the building.
The army's WP grenade is so effective it
is also used as an antipersonnel weapon
as well, which further detracts from its
use as a benign tool.

Mark needed a smoke device that would
produce clouds of smoke but not endanger
life or property by starting a fire.
Since nothing satisfactory was on the
market that was small enough, Mark
himself, along with Professor Haskins
developed one in the workshop of the
Stronghold.

The M-1 Smoke Ball is still under
development, and Mark hopes to utilize
a slightly heavier outer shell that will
contain higher pressure so more of the
compressed chemicals can be packed into
the container. Slightly larger than a
golf ball, but smaller than a tennis
ball, one of the Smoke Balls may be
carried in a jacket pocket without
attracting attention. The M-1 Smoke
Balls are not for sale.

Specifications

Size: 2.25 inches in diameter

Surface shell: Slightly roughened for grip and contact

Body shell: Joined hemispheres of highly frangible, low-impact plastic

Color code: Light blue color, indicating smoke only

Filler: Secret formula that erupts into thick bluish smoke when chemicals are exposed to ambient air

Operation: Hand thrown. The breakable plastic functions well against plaster walls, wooden floors, cement, stucco, almost any hard surface except single-strength window glass or carpets and other soft substances.

Performance

The M-1 Smoke Ball is a low-key offensive weapon designed to cause the least possible damage when used in friendly territory. It cannot cause a fire, and the smoke is benign and will not irritate the skin or damage drapes, furnishings, or paint. There is no residual odor left once a complete airing is accomplished.

The Smoke Ball is used primarily for flushing out a barricaded suspect in structures where no fire is wanted. They

work best in small rooms ten-to-twelve
feet square, in hallways, vehicles, etc.
Their main advantage is in their antifire
characteristic, which allows them to be
used in many buildings where Mark would
not use white phosphorus. The M-1 is
under continuing development so a more
effective smoke ball may be produced.

RESISTWEVE CLOTH

For years lawmen and dictators alike
have searched for the ideal bullet-proof
vest, one that would be lightweight,
compact, and yet effective. None had
been invented, and police struggle with
the heavier but effective models now on
the market.

Early in his career, the Penetrator
realized the need for something better,
and after testing all products available,
searched out a specialist in Newport
Beach, California, who had published a
paper on his continuing research into a
little known area that he called bullet-
proof cloth. The Penetrator urged the
man to finish his work, supplied him
with funding, and in the end the man
produced a fabulous material called
Resistweve cloth.

A sport jacket made of this material
is no heavier than a regular sport
jacket; yet it can stop a .38 slug or

anything smaller at nearly point-blank range at anything other than a ninety-degree angle of fire at the point of impact. A perpendicular shot would penetrate the fabric but would have little power left and probably would not puncture the skin.

The inventor began with a special thin fabric woven from tough Kevlar synthetic fiber used in tire cords and a fine metallic thread. The ultrathin weave cloth was then heat bonded together into a three-layer sandwich with the heavier vertical threads in each layer crossing each other at ninety degrees, much as the wood grain does in plywood. Next, two of these three-layer sandwiches were put together with a newly developed flexible fabric adhesive that bonds and stretches on impact. The six-layer fabric has an amazing antipenetration property.

The six plies in finished form are slightly thicker than the material in a good wool shirt. Three such thicknesses of the six-ply basic material are used to make the sport jackets. The basic material forms shirts and pants.

Specifications

Resistweve: 6-to-18 ply/laminated cloth
Content: Kevlar fiber and metallic
            threads woven

| Form: | Cloth about as thick as a wool shirt. Produced in a wide variety of colors and patterns. Two weights only: one for shirts and pants, one for jackets. No usual style vests are made. |
| Evaluation: | Dramatic bullet-stopping properties. Transmits much of bullet's impact power into surrounding cloth, which helps spread the shock over a wide area. Bruises result from any bullet strike. Possibility of broken ribs exist, but so far Mark has had no penetration of the jacket or the shirt or pants by fired rounds. |

PENETRATOR'S BLUE-FLINT ARROWHEAD

The Penetrator's trademark, his sign, is a 2.5-inch chipped, blue-flint arrowhead. The arrowheads are authentic, made by Indians, in the old method of painstakingly chipping small flakes of flint off with a rock-type hammer until the flint is formed in the shape wanted. Since these arrowheads are made by hand, no two of them are exactly the same.

The arrowheads are big game heads,

used for killing deer, antelope, buffalo, and bear by early Cheyenne hunters.

The Penetrator uses this trademark as a warning to criminals, as an announcement to others that he is in the area, and often as a signal to the press that he is in town and that the more articles and stories they print about him and his devastating effect on criminals the better. In his way Mark puts the target on the defensive, makes him move so the Penetrator can do his work more easily.

Mark uses the arrowhead more sparingly now, since its presence informs the press but also pinpoints for the police and the FBI his location. He is wanted by many law enforcement agencies; yet he usually gets good press coverage wherever he goes. The newspapers seem to understand and accept his extralegal actions more easily than the police agencies.

The arrowheads are not for sale.

THE QUARTER STAFF

Occasionally Mark finds use for the quarter staff, a fighting stave, in some mission. It's nothing more than a stick about four feet long, but the skill in using it is much like fencing, and the Penetrator is an expert with this weapon.

One benefit of knowing this fighting technique is that any long piece of wood may be used as a fighting stave by simply adapting the length and weight to the types of blows and thrusts that are made.

Mark has used the quarter staff several times, including his fight with Preacher Mann, the deep-freeze expert in book Number 24, <u>Cryogenic Nightmare.</u>

Specifications

Length: 36 to 48 inches

Size: Preferably about an inch in diameter but any size easily held will perform the same function, just so the stick isn't too heavy

Material: South African hardwood makes the best kind, carved, not sawed or turned from a tree limb. It should be smoothed and sanded—then finished with a wood preservative but not with any gloss or shine that would become sweat-slippery.

Availability: Not generally sold in this country. Practice quarter staffs may be made from 3/4-inch dowling that is rounded on the ends. Buy from any lumber yard by the lineal foot. Costs from 48 cents to 78 cents per foot.

SECOND-SKIN GLOVES

Early in his career the Penetrator
realized that his fingerprints could be
his undoing. His prints were on file
with the army and could easily be matched
by a cross check with the FBI in
Washington.

A friend of Mark's found the answer:
Mark should wear a second skin over his
hands. Together they developed from
semipermeable plastic a second-skin glove
for the Penetrator. It was so lifelike
that you could shake hands with the
Penetrator and never know he had on
gloves. The plastic looked like Mark's
real hands, had raised veins, knuckles,
hair, and even small spots and blemishes.

The material they are made out of
is called semipermeable because its
structure allows the Penetrator's hands
to sweat and breathe through his normal
skin pores and out through the small
openings in the plastic. This also
permits the natural oils in the fingers
to escape and coat the false fingerprints
so they leave perfect sets of prints
for the police to lift.

However, when the police try to match
the prints, they get no matchups at all
since none of the prints or the fragments
are on file anywhere.

These ultimate weapons to help Mark
remain anonymous, the fingerprints were

carefully crafted by a skilled artist so
they were unique, so there would be no
possibility for any law agency to come
up with the "ten-point similarity"
requirement for a match. The prints are
scrambled from one set of gloves to the
next and offer an infinite number of
combinations. They are carefully
engraved, and the rings, grooves and
whorls are formed into the fingertips
of the gloves in such real life patterns
that they have been frustrating lawmen
for many years.

In some cases where Mark leaves
readable fingerprints, he burns the
gloves after use. At other times he uses
more than one pair of gloves on a
mission to confuse both the police and
the underworld bosses, who are often
hunting him as well with sophisticated
tactics.

As you can imagine, these gloves are
are so expensive to create and produce
not available for sale to anyone. They
that few persons but the Penetrator
would want to use them.

**Out of the American West rides a new hero.
He rides alone . . . trusting no one.**

SPECIAL PREVIEW

Edge *is not like other western novels. In a tradition-bound
genre long dominated by the heroic cowpoke, we now have
the western anti-hero, an un-hero . . . a character seemingly
devoid of any sympathetic virtues. "A mean, sub-bitchin,'
baad-ass!" For readers who were introduced to the western via
Fran Striker's Lone Ranger tales, and who have learned about
the ways of the American West from the countless volumes
penned by Max Brand and Zane Grey, the adventures of Edge
will be quite shocking. Without question, these are the most
violent and bloody stories ever written in this field. Only two
things are certain about Edge: first, he is totally unpredicta-
ble, and has no pretense of ethics or honor . . . for him there
is no Code of the West, no Rules of the Range. Secondly, since
the first book of Edge's adventures was published by Pinnacle
in July of 1972, the sales and reader reaction have continued
to grow steadily. Edge is now a major part of the western
genre, alongside ol' Max and Zane, and Louis L'Amour. But*

Edge *will never be confused with any of 'em, because* Edge *is an original, tough hombre who defies any attempt to be cleaned up, calmed-down or made honorable. And who is to say that* Edge *may not be a realistic portrayal of our early American West? Perhaps more authentic than we know.*

George G. Gilman created *Edge* in 1971. The idea grew out of an editorial meeting in a London pub. It was, obviously, a fortunate blending of concepts between writer and editor. Up to this point Mr. Gilman's career included stints as a newspaperman, short story writer, compiler of crossword puzzles, and a few not-too-successful mysteries and police novels. With the publication in England of his first *Edge* novel, *The Loner*, Mr. Gilman's writing career took off. British readers went crazy over them, likening them to the "spaghetti westerns" of Clint Eastwood. In October, 1971, an American editor visiting the offices of New English Library in London spotted the cover of the first book on a bulletin board and asked about it. He was told it was "A cheeky Britisher's incredibly gory attempt at developing a new western series." Within a few days Pinnacle's editor had bought the series for publication in the United States. "It was," he said, "the perfect answer to the staid old westerns, which are so dull, so predictable, and so all-alike."

The first reactions to *Edge* in New York were incredulous. "Too violent!" "It's too far from the western formula, fans won't accept it." "How the hell can a British writer write about *our* American West?" But Pinnacle's editors felt they had something hot, and that the reading public was ready for it. So they published the first two *Edge* books simultaneously; *The Loner* and *Ten Grand* were issued in July 1972.

But, just *who* is Edge? We'll try to explain. His name was Josiah Hedges, a rather nondescript, even innocent, monicker for the times. Actually we meet Josiah's younger brother, Jamie Hedges, first. It is 1865, in the state of Iowa, a peaceful farmstead. The Civil War is over and young Jamie is awaiting the return of his brother, who's been five years at war. Six hundred thousand others have died, but Josiah was coming home. All would be well again. Jamie could hardly contain his excitement. He wasn't yet nineteen.

The following is an edited version of the first few chapters, as we are introduced to Josiah Hedges:

* * *

Six riders appeared in the distance, it must be Josiah! But then Jamie saw something which clouded his face, caused him to reach down and press Patch's head against his leg, giving or seeking assurance.

"Hi there, boy, you must be Joe's little brother Jamie."

He was big and mean-looking and, even though he smiled as he spoke, his crooked and tobacco-browned teeth gave his face an evil cast. But Jamie was old enough to know not to trust first impressions: and the mention of his brother's name raised the flames of excitement again.

"You know Joe? I'm expecting him. Where is he?"

"Well, boy," he drawled, shuffling his feet. "Hell, when you got bad news to give, tell it quick is how I look at things. Joe won't be coming today. Not any day. He's dead, boy."

"We didn't only come to give you the news, boy," the sergeant said. "Hardly like to bring up another matter, but you're almost a man now. Probably are a man in everything except years—living out here alone in the wilderness like you do. It's money, boy.

"Joe died in debt, you see. He didn't play much poker, but when he did there was just no stopping him."

Liar, Jamie wanted to scream at them. *Filthy rotten liar*.

"Night before he died," the sergeant continued. "Joe owed me five hundred dollars. He wanted to play me double or nothing. I didn't want to, but your brother was sure a stubborn cuss when he wanted to be."

Joe never gambled. Ma and Pa taught us both good.

"So we played a hand and Joe was unlucky." His gaze continued to be locked on Jamie's, while his discolored teeth were shown in another parody of a smile. "I wasn't worried none about the debt, boy. See, Joe told me he'd been sending money home to you regular like."

"There ain't no money on the place and you're a lying son-ofabitch. Joe never gambled. Every cent he earned went into a bank so we could do things with this place. Big things. I don't even believe Joe's dead. Get off our land."

Jamie was held erect against this oak, secured by a length of rope that bound him tightly at ankles, thighs, stomach, chest, and throat; except for his right arm left free of the bonds so that it could be raised out and the hand fastened, fingers splayed over the tree trunk by nails driven between them and bent over. But Jamie gritted his teeth and looked back at Forrest defiantly, trying desperately to conceal the twisted terror that reached his very nerve ends.

"You got your fingers and a thumb on that right hand, boy," Forrest said softly. "You also got another hand and we got lots of nails. I'll start with the thumb. I'm good. That's why they made me platoon sergeant. Your brother recommended me, boy. I don't miss. Where's the money?"

The enormous gun roared and Jamie could no longer feel anything in his right hand. But Forrest's aim was true and when the boy looked down it was just his thumb that lay in the dust, the shattered bone gleaming white against the scarlet blood pumping from the still warm flesh. Then the numbness went and white hot pain engulfed his entire arm as he screamed.

"You tell me where the money is hid, boy," Forrest said, having to raise his voice and make himself heard above the sounds of agony, but still empty of emotion.

The gun exploded into sound again and this time there was no moment of numbness as Jamie's forefinger fell to the ground.

"Don't hog it all yourself, Frank," Billy Seward shouted, drawing his revolver. "You weren't the only crack shot in the whole damn war."

"You stupid bastard," Forrest yelled as he spun around. "Don't kill him. . . ."

But the man with the whiskey bottle suddenly fired from the hip, the bullet whining past Forrest's shoulder to hit Jamie squarely between the eyes, the blood spurting from the fatal wound like red mud to mask the boy's death agony. The gasps of the other men told Forrest it was over and his Colt spoke again, the bullet smashing into the drunken man's groin. He went down hard into a sitting position, dropping his gun, splaying his legs, his hands clenching at his lower abdomen.

"Help me, Frank, my guts are running out. I didn't mean to kill him."

"But you did," Forrest said, spat full into his face and brought up his foot to kick the injured man savagely on the jaw, sending him sprawling on to his back. He looked around at the others as, their faces depicting fear, they holstered their guns. "Burn the place to the ground," he ordered with low-key fury. "If we can't get the money, Captain damn Josiah C. Hedges ain't gonna find it, either."

Joe caught his first sight of the farm and was sure it was a trick of his imagination that painted the picture hanging before his eyes. But then the gentle breeze that had been coming from the south suddenly veered and he caught the acrid stench of smoke in his nostrils, confirming that the black smudges rising lazily upwards from the wide area of darkened country ahead was actual evidence of a fire.

As he galloped toward what was now the charred remains of the Hedges farmstead, Joe looked down at the rail, recognizing in the thick dust of a long hot summer signs of the recent passage of many horses—horses with shod hoofs. As he thundered up the final length of the trail, Joe saw only two areas of movement, one around the big oak and another some yards distant, toward the smouldering ruins of the house, and as he reined his horse at the gateway he slid the twelve shot Henry repeater from its boot and leapt to the ground, firing from hip level. Only one of the evil buzz that had been tearing ferociously at dead human flesh escaped, lumbering with incensed screeches into the acrid air.

For perhaps a minute Joe stood unmoving, looking at Jamie bound to the tree. He knew it was his brother, even though his face was unrecognizable where the scavengers had ripped the flesh to the bone. He saw the right hand picked almost completely clean of flesh, as a three fingered skeleton of what it had been, still securely nailed to the tree. He took hold of Jamie's shirt front and ripped it, pressed his lips against the cold, waxy flesh of his brother's chest, letting his grief escape, not moving until his throat was pained by dry sobs and his tears were exhausted. . . .

"Jamie, our ma and pa taught us a lot out of the Good Book, but it's a long time since I felt the need to know about such things. I guess you'd know better than me what to say at a time like this. Rest easy, brother, I'll settle your score. Whoever they are and wherever they run, I'll find them and I'll kill them. I've learned some special ways of killing people and I'll avenge you good." Now Joe looked up at the sky, a bright sheet of azure cleared of smoke. "Take care of my kid brother, Lord," he said softly, and put on his hat with a gesture of finality, marking the end of his moments of graveside reverence. Then he went to the pile of blackened timber, which was the corner of what had been Jamie's bedroom. Joe used the edge of the spade to prise up the scorched floor boards. Beneath was a tin box containing every cent of the two thousand dollars Joe had sent home from the war, stacked neatly in piles of one, five, and ten dollar bills.

Only now, more than two hours since he had returned to the farmstead, did Joe cross to look at the second dead man.

The scavenging birds had again made their feast at the man-made source of blood. The dead man lay on his back, arms and legs splayed. Above the waist and below the thighs he was unmarked, the birds content to tear away his genitals and rip a gaping hole in his stomach, their talons and bills delving inside to drag out the intestines, the uneaten portions of which now trailed in the dust. . . .

Then Joe looked at the face of the dead man and his cold eyes narrowed. The man was Bob Rhett, he recalled. He had fought a drunken coward's war, his many failings covered by his platoon sergeant Frank Forrest. So they were the five men who must die . . . Frank Forrest, Billy Seward, John Scott, Hal Douglas, and Roger Bell. They were inseparable throughout the war.

Joe walked to his horse and mounted. He had not gone fifty yards before he saw a buzzard swoop down and tug at something that suddenly came free. Then it rose into the air with an ungainly flapping of wings, to find a safer place to enjoy its prize. As it wheeled away, Joe saw that swinging from its bill were the entrails of Bob Rhett.

Joe grinned for the first time that day, an expression of cold slit eyes and bared teeth that utterly lacked humor. "You never did have any guts, Rhett," he said aloud.

* * *

From this day of horror Josiah Hedges forged a new career as a killer. A killer of the worst kind, born of violence, driven by revenge. As you'll note in the preceding material, Edge often shows his grim sense of irony, a graveyard humor. Edge is not like anyone you've met in fact or fiction. He is without doubt the most cold-bloodedly violent character to ever roam the West. You'll hate him, you'll cringe at what he does, you'll wince at the explicit description of all that transpires . . . and you'll come back for more.

7 Best-Selling War Books

From the Spanish Civil War . . .

Men in Battle, by Alvah Bessie
☐ P40-037-8 $1.95

"A true, honest, fine book. Bessie writes truly and finely of all that he could see . . . and he saw enough." —Ernest Hemingway

To World War II . . .

Gold from Crete, by C. S. Forester
☐ 230960-7 $1.50

Ten tales of courage and danger on the high seas by C. S. Forester, author of the renowned adventures of Horatio Hornblower.

The Deep Six, by Martin Dibner,
author of *The Trouble with Heroes*
☐ 240958-5 $1.75

"[I] rank Mr. Dibner's novels alongside the great novels about the Navy, *The Caine Mutiny,* and *The Cruel Sea,* for he has honestly reflected life at sea in wartime . . . a fine book, a moving novel."
                —San Francisco Chronicle

The Race for Rome, by Dan Kurzman
☐ P40-013-0 $2.50

"A book that does for Rome what *Is Paris Burning?* did for Paris . . . compelling reading." —Publishers Weekly

The Bravest Battle, by Dan Kurzman
☐ P40-182-5 $2.50

"Monumental and awe-inspiring, this is the definitive story . . . an epic of human fervor, will, and endurance."   —Meyer Levin

Blue Skies and Blood: The Battle of the Coral Sea
by Edwin P. Hoyt
☐ 240907-0 $1.75

The stirring true story of steel ships and iron men in the first aircraft-carrier battle in history—and the greatest sea battle of World War II.

To Vietnam . . .

Sand in the Wind, by Robert Roth
☐ 40-060-2 $2.25

"*Sand in the Wind* may just become the *All Quiet on the Western Front* or *The Naked and the Dead* of the Vietnam conflict."
                —King Features Syndicate

PINNACLE—BOOK MAILING SERVICE, Box 690, Rockville Centre, N.Y. 11571

Please send me the books I have checked above. I am enclosing $ _____ (please add 50¢ to cover postage and handling). Send check or money order—no cash or C.O.D.'s please.

Name _____

Address_____

City _____ State/Zip _____

Please allow approximately four weeks for delivery.